The Naga Story

A Novel

SUMAN BAJPAI

Published by
PRABHAT PRAKASHAN PVT. LTD.
4/19 Asaf Ali Road,
New Delhi-110 002 (INDIA)
e-mail: prabhatbooks@gmail.com

ISBN 978-93-5562-133-7

THE NAGA STORY
by Suman Bajpai

Edition
First, 2024

Price
₹ 350.00 (Rupees Three Hundred Fifty only)

Printed at
S.S. Japan Art, Delhi

Dedicated to

those religion-protecting Naga sadhus,

who have been engaged in public welfare for centuries

and who meditate with deep concentration

in some cave or on a mountain.

Introduction

The life of Naga Sadhus is one of austerity. A mystery, a curiosity, a wonder—many questions arise when it comes to Naga Sadhus. Whenever the Kumbh and Ardh Kumbh Mela take place in the country, Naga Sadhus are seen. For centuries, Naga Sadhus have been viewed with both faith and a sense of mystery and wonder. There is no doubt that they are a subject of astonishment for the public because their attire, activities, and methods of meditation are out of the ordinary. No one can predict when they might be pleased or when they might get angry.

Naga Sadhus, with their long dreadlocks and ash-covered naked bodies, have no connection with the outside world. Their lives are filled with hardships that common people cannot even imagine. Living a highly disciplined and ascetic life in some cave, meditating, these Naga Sadhus are beyond joy and sorrow as we may know it.

The tradition of Naga Sadhus is not new; it has been going on for thousands of years. We find signs of this tradition in the coins and images of Mohenjo-Daro, where Naga Sadhus are seen worshipping Lord Shiva in the form of Pashupati Nath. It is said that when Alexander and his soldiers came to India, they encountered Naga Sadhus. Not only that, but Lord Buddha and

Lord Mahavira were also greatly influenced by the austerity and dedication of the Naga Sadhus towards their motherland.

The current form of the Indian Sanatan Dharma was established by Adi Guru Shankaracharya. Shankar was born in mid-8th century, a time when the state and direction of the Indian populace was in turmoil. Many invaders, attracted by India's wealth, were making their way to the subcontinent. Some took away its treasures, while others were so enchanted by India's divine aura that they stayed.

Peace and order was disrupted. God, religion, and religious scriptures faced all kinds of challenges—logical, martial, and scholarly. In such times, Shankaracharya established Sanatan Dharma to safeguard the way of life. One important step was the construction of the four Peethas (spiritual centers) at the four corners of the country. Adi Guru initiated the establishment of akharas (armed branches of various sects of Sanatan Dharma) to counter those who looted the properties of monasteries and temples and harassed the devotees.

In that era of social turmoil, Adi Guru Shankaracharya felt that merely spiritual power was not enough to face these challenges. He emphasized that young Sadhus should strengthen their bodies through exercise and also acquire proficiency in handling weapons. Hermitages were established where such exercises or weapon training were conducted, which later came to be known as 'akharas.' Shankaracharya suggested that these akharas use force if necessary to protect monasteries, temples, and devotees. Thus, during the period of external invasions, these akharas acted as a protective shield.

Many times, local kings and princes sought the assistance of Naga warrior Sadhus in the face of foreign invasions. History records several glorious battles in which more than forty thousand Naga warriors participated. They were called 'Dharma Rakshak Yoddhas' (protectors of religion).

After India's independence, these akharas abandoned their military character. Their life is not easy, yet there are still many misconceptions about them. People in society do not know that whenever religion was in danger, they became warriors to protect it. They put down the scriptures and took up arms. When they become Naga Sadhus through intense penance, they dedicate their entire lives to the protection of religion and the welfare of people.

In this book, I have made a strong effort to interestingly portray the life and warrior aspect of Naga Sadhus. I have highlighted their contributions so that people can understand their valuable presence in our culture. I hope that after reading this book, people's perceptions of them will change, and their names will also be recorded in history books.

—Suman Bajpai

M: 9810795705

Author's Note

They were running frantically; their anger evident at the speed at which they were running. Strange and terrible sounds were coming out of their mouths as if they were running with a resolve that today they would not let any catastrophe befall. The chants of 'Har Har Mahadev' could be heard everywhere. There face was full with tangled beard and matted hair, and their eyes were red. Rudraksh garlands around their arms and neck, garlands made of marigold flowers wrapped around their neck and waist, kajal in the eyes, vermillion and sandalwood paste on their forehead. They carried tongs, a trident, damru in their hands whereas some even had kamandals in their hands.

Not a thread or cloth was on their body. In the name of apparel, they only had a piece of loincloth. With ashes smeared on their bodies, not one or two but countless Naga Sadhus were running towards one direction. It seemed as if a turmoil was occurring amidst high tides in a sea, and the flow was so strong that a fierceness could be experienced. Where was the half-naked sadhu running to, covered in ashes and chants of Har Har Mahadev?

The sight was such that it sent tremors through the heart. Countless thoughts were emerging in mind, about what was happening. It was a terrifying scene.

People in our country are unaware of the contributions of the Naga Sadhus to our culture and our traditions, and they foster views on the basis of their strange appearance. But the Naga Sadhus are the ultimate truth and there is no truth greater than them in the entire universe.

They are true and a manifestation of the soul and there is no cloth on the soul. Their body itself is the cloth because they themselves are souls. Their soul, like cloth, works as their apparel. People fail to understand the Nagas. They smear dust and mud on their body and wear the Rudraksha beads. The ash that they smear comes from dead bodies and if they cannot find it, they smear ashes from the Havana, because it also induces sacrifice.

The one who becomes a Naga, is free from this world. He is not a part of this world even though he lives in it. Nagas are considered to be the avatar (manifestation) of Shiva.

Naga Sadhus never travel during the day because the society is not able to understand and accept them. But still, a glance of Naga Sadhus arises curiosity in everybody's minds. When these Naga Sadhus, who outshine even women with their adornments, appear in lakhs during the Maha Kumbh, the thought of knowing more and more about them definitely comes to all of us at least once. During Kumbh, these Sadhus suddenly become a symbol of mysticism. Traditionally, the life of a Naga Sadhu is one of meditation, penance and renunciation and it is only during Kumbh that they appear in public.

The life of Naga Sadhus dancing, singing, jumping, playing Damru-Dafli, carrying Trishul-Tongs, remains an unsolved mystery for humans even today when so much progress has been made, because perhaps they themselves do not want people to know more about their lives.

Contents

Introduction 5

Author's Note 9

1. A Step into the World of Solitude 13

2. The Meeting 21

3 Process of becoming a Naga Sadhu 27

4 Seeking Alms 35

5 Ashes and Asceticism 41

6 Kirat's Diary 46

7 Alexander's Pride is Shattered 53

8 Questions and Answers 62

9 History Scholar Professor Vachaspati 71

10 Role of the Akharas 79

11 Abdali's Invasions 87

12 The Sacrifices that are not Recorded on Paper 96

13 War against the Mughals 104

14 Protecting the Vishawanath Temple 113

15	Far too many Struggles	121
16	Naga Sadhvis	129
17	Meeting with the Mahant	139
18	Ash from the Crematorium	151
19	The Ultimate Goal - Salvation	161
20	The Glory of Kumbh	171
21	The Sadhus Deserve Respect	179

1.
A Step into the World of Solitude

"What were you thinking that you came here? You are young, maybe that's why you have wandered off to here, in search of some thrill! Go back at once. This world is not meant for you and we do not allow any body to enter into our world," a loud voice echoed.

At the moment they stood inside a cave where it was dark everywhere and it was impossible to know where the voice was coming from and whom it belonged to. Gradually the eyes adapted to the darkness. It seemed a beam of faint light erupted. Perhaps that beam was entering through a slit. They felt some roughness under their feet. At some places it was slippery due to which they stumbled while walking. The stone structures on the walls seemed to be of strange and bizarre shapes. Sometimes they looked artistic and sometimes scary. At some places, a structure like the hood of Sheshnaga was visible on the stones. A question knocked on the mind, is the earth resting on this?

They moved forward slowly so that they could reach the source of the voice. Often, harsh and crackling sound would come from beneath the feet that it would seem that they were walking on someone's bones. The shape of Kaal Bhairav's tongue appeared on the wall in front. A little further, Garuda with a bent neck was seen sitting on top of a pond. So, did Shiva do penance here? They were surprised that despite being so deep inside the ground, they were not feeling suffocated in the cave, rather they were feeling an unprecedented calm.

They had heard a lot about this place and that was why they came here, even though they knew that it would not be easy to reach here. They had not cared for any difficulties in their way and had come here. It has been rightly said that curiosity and inquisitiveness overpower a person in such a way that he is not afraid of the consequences. They had heard that the severed head of Lord Ganesh is kept in this cave and statues like Sheshnaga are also found here. Lord Shiva resides here; they had heard it from the people.

"Shall we go back? Anyway you will not be able to click photographs here, it is so dark," the girl said to the young man who had a camera strap on his shoulders.

"You too will not be able to write anything without the light. It seems the pages of your diary will remain blank." He whispered with a soft laughter. "By the way what does your study so far tell us about this place?"

A smile appeared on the lips of the girl. She was holding a diary in her hand which had a blue cover and a pen kept in between its pages was protruded.

Unable to determine the direction of the voice, they both stood there and leaned against the wall. Actually, they were in a dilemma, whether to move forward or return back! The fearless resolve with which they had come here was shaken a bit.

"It would not be right to return after coming so far and facing so many difficulties. Would it be right to let our efforts go in vain? It is better to stay here until the eyes get accustomed to the darkness. Nothing will happen, I am with you," the young man assured the girl.

"But the voice that has ordered us to return back, how did it know that we are young? Can they see us? Why can we not see anybody? Haven't we really come into some mysterious world?" said the girl and the young man held her hand tightly.

"Uncovering mysteries is your subject. Then why are you nervous? You have a lot of knowledge. Tell me something about this place," the young man said with the intention of diverting the girl's attention.

"I cannot say with full confidence that this is the same cave that I have read about, but it seems to be the same to a large extent. According to the Puranas, this mysterious cave was discovered by King Rituparna in the Treta Yuga, after which he met the King of the Nagas, Adhishesha. King Adhishesha took King Rituparna inside the cave, where he saw all the gods and goddesses and Lord Shiva. It is also said that King Rituparna was the first human to discover it. After the Treta Yuga, mention of this cave was found in the Dwapar Yuga when the Pandavas rediscovered this cave and they used to stay here and worship Lord Shiva. According to mythology, in Kali Yuga, it was discovered by Adi Shankaracharya in the eighth century. Even then, sages used to meditate here... they had made it a living place as if..."

"Have you not left yet?" The same voice echoed again. This time it seemed as if there was fire in the voice. "Why have you come here?"

The young man was terrified for a moment due to the roar in the voice. Now it was coming from somewhere nearby. A yellow light was trembling on the floor and walls of the cave.

It seemed like a burning flame which was casting its shadow. Maybe it is the light of a lantern. A single hermit was standing before them. His leg started shaking when he saw his red fiery eyes. Long beard, ash covering his body and in the name of attire, just a loincloth. He sat cross legged on the floor. Anybody could get frightened at first sight upon seeing that figure sitting there.

The young man looked around him. Now he could see, although not very clearly but at least he could see to understand the sight before him. Many other sadhus were sitting there. All of them were almost naked, smeared in ashes, a red tilak on their forehead, garland of Rudraksh in their neck. A mini trident tied in their hairlocks and tongs kept nearby.

Some sadhus were engrossed in meditation, some in penance. Some seemed to be meditating silently. Those sadhus were meditating in the icy solitude and in the bone-chilling cold. Long matted locks were wrapped around their heads. Despite the cold, there was no tremor on their bodies, as if the firmness of their minds had made the bodies inert. The eyes of other sadhus were closed, but looking at them it seemed that if they opened, they would burn them to ashes. Their faces were rough, their entire existence was unperturbed, neutral, free from worldly troubles...

Anyone would think twice before stepping into this world of solitude but those who are passionate and courageous know no fear. There was a conviction to do something different, which was visible on the young man's face. The fear that had crept in him a few moments ago had now vanished. The same was true for the girl, she too was determined along with the young man. Were they a couple in love who had wandered into these caves while roaming? Did they not know that it was prohibited for ordinary people to come here? Have they thought about the punishment for disturbing the meditation of these ascetics or has some quest brought them here?

That young man composed himself. What should he tell a reason for his arrival? When he could not think of anything, he said with determination "I want to be part of your world." He remained silent for a few moments. A state of confusion had gripped him. The girl nudged him, as if to alert him to think before saying anything.

"What do you mean?" the voice echoed throughout the cave with a terrifying noise.

In a hurry, the young man blurted out, "I want to become a Naga Sadhu." His hands folded in front of the Sadhu.

"Haha…haha…a loud laughter spread all around. This echo was not of just one person, many voices were involved in it. The sages sitting in the posture of meditation had opened their eyes. They got up and came near the young man. Some had lanterns in their hands and some had candles. No one had anything on their body except ashes. They were completely naked. It was a frightening sight. The girl lowered her eyes.

The boy was wearing jeans and a t-shirt and a jacket over it. The girl, whose height was exactly the same as the boy, that is, around five feet eight inches, was very beautiful. She was fair-skinned and had a slender body. Due to her height, she looked even taller than the boy. The boy had a full body and a round face.

Both of them looked complementary to each other and were also full of confidence. That girl was also wearing jeans, very tight jeans and a tight top. She was also wearing a black jacket.

"If you want to become like us then also answer this - have you left your world behind you or have you brought it with you? Is she your companion?"

The anger of that middle-aged sage was at its peak, but he knew how to control it.

"She has also left her world and come here. She also wants to become a Naga Sadhvi." This time the young man's eyes had a strange glitter while talking. He had himself decided for the girl, without giving it a thought whether she agrees to it or not.

"Do you even know what you are saying? Youngsters like you don't even know how to think seriously. You are deciding everything for this girl on your own?

Have you even asked her what she wants? Do you even know what it means to become a Naga Sadhu or Sadhvi? Don't waste our time. I am saying this again, go away from here. We don't like to meet anyone. This is our world, in which entry of other people is prohibited."

"The way you live here, I mean both of us want to experience that life," the young man spoke in an excited tone, in his own tune. As if he had not heard what the sadhu said. He lacks patience!

The girl was looking at him in surprise. She remained silent, not wanting to create a situation of unnecessary dispute.

"Our life is not something to be experienced or experimented. This is a tough penance," the Sadhu's eyes had lit up like fire.

"Becoming a Naga Sadhu is not a joke, nor is it a game that you play for a few days, have fun and then return to your world. It is not something like your love which goes away after sometime. Our life is a difficult test. We have to spend our entire life with our feet firmly planted on the hard ground. That too without any regret or remorse in our mind, because we choose this life voluntarily."

"But we really want to adopt your life. We will do whatever you say." The young man seemed to have become adamant.

"Enough is enough. Leave this place immediately or else you will lose your life. If you want to leave your world, do so, but your entry into our world is prohibited. Young men like you have made life a joke. Why do you want to ruin this girl's life along with yours? Our world is not like your world. This is a very difficult path, which is not possible for young men like you to walk on. This is not your urban culture's lifestyle, which you can change at will whenever you want or follow indiscipline. Do whatever you want, act according to your will, such freedom is not available here. Our lifestyle is bound by rules and discipline. There is no scope for even the slightest laxity in it. Our way of living is more difficult than the harsh penance. You must have come here thinking that there must be some hippie community or common sadhus who are doing penance in the cave here, but we are Naga Sadhus. We live naked, but strict conduct and self-control are our cover. You are a fool. Go away from here. Do you have the courage to perform your own pind-daan (a ritual performed for dead people)? Your companion, who has come here with you, is more foolish than you."

The sadhu remained silent for a few moments, then looking at the girl said, "I can understand that you have come with him blinded by his love. But a delicate girl like you, who believes only love to be the truth of life, will be able to live among us, like us? Go away immediately. We have to go and beg for alms."

All the Naga Sadhus got ready to leave.

❑

2.
The Meeting

"We do not intend to disrupt your penance or discipline. We will leave, but we have come from very far away, so will it be right to return without knowing about you? If I cannot become a Naga Sadhu, then you will have to give me some reason for it." The young man's courage amazed the sages. They understood that he is not going to return easily and that he has not come here to become a Naga Sadhu. Both of them had come here to know about them and take their photographs just like tourists. It was possible that they were travelling and had wandered off to that place while walking.

"The curiosity in me after witnessing the Kumbh Mela made me a bit too wise. I wanted to meet you there itself but it was crowded, therefore I was waiting for the mela to get over, and then talk to you in peace but as soon as the Kumbh Mela was over, you guys disappeared God knows where." The young man had slowly started to speak his mind.

"We shall leave, but if you could tell us something about you, about the culture of Naga Sadhus, about their lifestyle and customs….", the girl spoke this time. Apart from the hesitation, there was a request in her tone.

"Sit down," suddenly an elderly sadhu appeared before them and spoke. "We do not talk to anyone. We have no relations with worldly affairs, but since you have come this far, I think I should introduce you to the truth of Naga Sadhus. I will tell you about our history. This will clear your misunderstandings as well as your doubts and you will never dare to come back here again."

He sat right in front of them. It seemed that he was the oldest among the other sadhus present there and it was quite possible that he was their leader because no one opposed what he said. Stroking his long white beard and adjusting the trident on his matted locks, he started explaining, "The word 'Naga' is very old. It is derived from the Sanskrit word 'Nag' which means mountains. The people who live there are known as Pahadis (from the word pahad) or Nagas. Naga also refers to people who remain naked. The Naga dynasty and Naga caste have a very old history in India. Many ascetic sects and traditions are believed to have started from the Shaiva sect. We carry trident, conch, sword and light a fire. We are staunch followers of the Shaiva sect and are strict about our rules. Many of us are Siddhas and many are Aughars."

"Aughar? But aren't they different? They live in crematorium perhaps…"

"Often Naga Sadhus and Aghoris are considered to be the same, but you will be surprised to know that there is as much difference between these two as there is between day and night, earth and sky...."

"Tell us something about the Aghoris as well?" the girl asked. She was aslo noting down his words in her diary.

"Why are you writing all this?" The old sadhu roared.

"So that I remember," she said in a trembling voice. She had hidden the real thing. Perhaps there was no point in telling it or it could be told, but she remained silent.

"Hmm! But first learn about the Naga Sadhus." Said the old man in a harsh tone. Then he mellowed down and said to another Sadhu, "Put a lantern in front of them. They seem to be some special kind of stubborn youngsters. You guys sit down."

The young man and the girl sat down at once. When they have been asked to sit, it means he will definitely tell something.

"If you have been to Kumbh mela then you must be aware that the crowd of Naga Sadhus gathers only in Maha Kumbh, Ardha - Kumbh or Simhastha - Kumbh and as soon as the Kumbh ends, they disappear overnight, as you also just mentioned. Everybody wonders where they go. Nobody knows where they come from and where they go to… just that a storm of crowd appears and as soon as the waves calm down, they disappear. After the Kumbh ends, most of the sadhus wrap their bodies with ash and go to the peaks of the Himalayas. There they do rigorous penance at their Guru's place till the next Kumbh. During this penance, they survive by eating fruits and flowers only. Due to doing rigorous penance for years, their hair becomes several meters long and this penance is completed only when they take a dip in the Ganga during the Kumbh Mela."

"The same thing had happened then," the young man said. "When I went to Ujjain, they had disappeared suddenly. After making a strong presence and identity of Simhastha, after opening the wonder land for the people, after taking the last royal bath (Shahi Snan), when did they leave Ujjain in the night? It is a mystery. The sudden disappearance of thousands of Naga Sadhus, who were the pride of Simhastha for a month, is a surprising thing."

Hearing this, the old man laughed and said, “Indeed we are like a puzzle for the common people, difficult to solve, an enigma, otherwise you would not have been so interested to know about us? Naga Sadhus travel through the forest paths. Usually we start walking late at night. During the journey, we do not go to any village or city, but camp in the forest and deserted paths. Due to this traveling at night and resting in the forest during the day, no one can sight us coming or going to Simhastha. Some Naga Sadhus go out in groups, while some travel alone. We consume roots, fruits, flowers and leaves during the journey and sleep on the ground itself.

“Most of the Naga Sadhus of the Akharas live in the Himalayas, Kashi, Gujarat and Uttarakhand. All of them do penance in the mountains, caves and caverns away from the village or city. Naga Sadhus change their place after living in a cave for a few years. We like to stay away from the contact of people.”

“Any special reason to do so?”

“Reason? Can a simple human understand us? The society is not ready even to accept us because it does not hold knowledge to understand us,” said the tall sadhu in an angry tone.

“Calm down Gajanan. Do not be perturbed by their questions. They have no fault in it. The world of Naga Sadhus has always been filled with more curiosity than questions. The curiosity that what is the truth of the strange world of Naga Sadhus? From where do so many sadhus come together at once? The question is where do these sadhus go to after their holy bath? Ask, what else do you want to know?” The old sadhu asked.

“Why do Naga Sadhus abandon their clothes and make the sky their cloths? Why do they smear ashes from dhuni over their entire body in the name of clothing?” This question was asked by the girl.

"Why do they live naked? This same question strikes the minds of many people when they see us. The truth is that as soon as you hear the term Naga Sadhu, the first thing you imagine is naked sadhus with ash smeared al over their bodies and that too in a negative way. Some people may find them uncivilized and religious fanatics. In reality Naga Sadhus give importance to nature and the natural state and therefore do not wear anything. Apart from this it is our belief that a person is born naked and this is why Naga Sadhus are always naked. Naga Sadhus smear ashes on their bodies and keep matted hair."

"Most people do not know that Naga Sadhus are a holy army of foot soldiers that protects Hinduism and who do not charge any money for it. Be it the Islamic invaders or the British expansionists, Naga Sadhus are always ready to protect Hinduism. We consider ourselves lucky to protect Hinduism but the irony is that the society does not remember our sacrifices ever nor is it grateful. Neither are we respected nor do we get a place in history books."

"It is believed that you are the staunch disciples of Shiva. Is it really true?" the young man asked with amazement.

"We are the ones on whose shoulders the Adi Guru Shankaracharya had entrusted the responsibility to protect the Sanatan Dharma. We are his roar, the trumpet of war that has been playing since centuries. But the disciples of Shiva, who the world knows as Naga Sadhus, don't just make war cries. They are expert in using weapons and show their skills by using weapons in occasions like the Mahakumbha.

"Naga Sadhus are experts in wielding all kinds of weapons. They are experts in every skill of weaponry along with the knowledge of scriptures. There is no mercy if they get angry otherwise even while remaining calm Naga Sadhus give a sense of amazing warrior. What does a saint got to do with weapons? But for us Naga Sadhus, our dressing is not complete without weapons. Our gods reside in weapons only. In simple terms, If Akharas are the force then Naga Sadhus are the commandos. History changed, systems changed, even the attitude the akharas have changed, but something which has not changed is the love of Naga Sadhus for their weapons. Even today it gives a testimony of the history of centuries.

"But this can also be not denied that the world of Naga Sadhus attracts the curiosity of the common people and this is the reason that just like you they too have a long list of questions for the Naga Sadhus. Anyway, that would be enough, now we need to go and you too should leave now. Do not disturb our meditation and do not seek to know too much. We need to go to seek alms. There was a sudden change in the tone of that elderly sage."

The young man and the girl looked at them in bewilderment. Now they did nothing wrong, then why did he get so angry?

❑

3
Process of becoming a Naga Sadhu

The young man did not budge. He looked at the Naga Sadhu right in his eyes. This time there was no fear in his eyes.

"Let's go. Why are you being so stubborn?" The girl tried to pull him by his arms. "They need to go seek alms, why are you unnecessarily getting adamant?"

"Wait Rumi. I will not leave until I get answers to my questions."

"They have already said enough, what else is there to know? And why are you so interested? It is I who should be interested. You are being adamant for nothing. Let us go Shekhar". The girl pleaded. She whispered in his ears, "and it is not that you want to become a Naga Sadhu, so why are you acting like it? This is not your theatre."

"Why are you in such a hurry to leave? There is still so much to know. And you too were so excited to know about them. You are doing research on them and yet want to return without knowing more? We have come this far; I will not return empty handed. If they think that we cannot become a part of their world then they will have to explain the reason for this and they will have to tell about their lives in detail."

“Don’t be childish,” Another elderly sage said this time. His voice was stern, yet it was said in a tone to make him understand. “And what is this theatre this girl was talking about? Do you work in theatres?”

The young man was embarrassed, he said “Yes, I am an actor. I direct as well as act in dramas. I am associated with theatre. By profession I am an engineer. Theatre is my hobby.”

“Very impressive! This is why you were able to act so well that you want to become a Naga Sadhu. Have a seat.” A middle-aged Sadhu, who was standing at the back, came forward and spoke. “We shall go to beg alms a little late but first let us quench the curiosity of this young man or else his mind will keep wandering and he won’t be able to return to his world. I don’t want this girl to pay for his stupidities who has come along with him without giving it a proper thought. This girl is in love and we will respect that. We are the protectors of dharma therefore we cannot witness any wrongdoings.”

The young man sat down and the girl also sat very close to him. All the sadhu sat down as well. “Being late is against our rules but if everybody agrees, then it is all right.” Said the sadhu who had initially ordered them to return. There was silence for a few moments.

“Please pacify his curiosity,” the middle-aged sadhu said to the another elderly sadhu.

“Perhaps you people think that becoming a Naga Sadhu is as simple as becoming any other sadhu, but it is not so.” He lit his chillum while glowering at the young man. “The truth is that we have to go through arduous tests to become a Naga Sadhu. No one can become a Naga Sadhu just like that, therefore in order to become a Naga Sadhu one has to enter the 'Guru – Shishya Parampara'. Has to stand under a banyan tree for six months. Has to serve his guru and do rigorous penance for years, only then can one attain the status of a Naga Sadhu. The process to make a Naga Sadhu begins during the Mahakumbh but it is not possible for everybody to become a Naga. It takes extreme conviction and strong desire to live the life of a sage to become a naga Sadhu. Nagas have to become different from the normal world and lead an unusual life.

"To carry forward the traditions of Sanatan and to protect Dharma at any cost, a process of becoming Naga Sadhu is adopted during every Mahakumbh by different 'Sanyasi Akharas'. There are 13 such akharas all across India, where Sanyasis are transformed in Nagas but of all these, 'Juna Akhara' is one such place which trains maximum number of Naga Sadhus.

"Normally only men older than eighteen years are made Nagas. Whenever a person approaches any akhara to become a sage, he is not admitted directly to the akhara. At first the akhara conducts its own investigation to determine why that person wants to become a Sadhu? A thorough background check for that person and his family is done. Then he is introduced to the difficulties in the life of a Naga Sadhu and his self-control is also tested.

"If the Akhara feels that man is suitable to become a Sadhu, only then is he granted permission to enter the akhara. He has to serve his guru for three years after getting entry to the akhara. He has to understand all the rituals and become part of them. After his admission in the akhara, he is taught about celibacy. He is made to observe celibacy for a very long time. Not only the physical control but his mental control is tested as well. His penance, celibacy, detachment, meditation, renunciation and discipline and devotion to religion are primarily tested. No one is given diksha suddenly. First it is determined if the person taking the diksha is free of all kinds of lusts and desires or not. It important to have a sense of service along with the vow of celibacy in the person wanting to take the diksha. It is believed that one who is becoming a Naga, is doing so for service and protection of dharma, nation and human kind.

"It is important to perform one's own pind-daan (last rites) before one can take the diksha. The first step in becoming a Naga Sadhu is to learn about celibacy. After completing it successfully, mahapurush Diksha can be imparted. It is followed by thread ceremony. After all this, they perform the last rites of their own self as well their family, this process is called 'Bijwaan'."

"They perform 17 last rites in which they perform 16 rites for their family members and 17th is for their own self. After performing their last rites, they declare themselves dead and it considered the end of their present life. After these last rites all the signs of their past life including thread ceremony, gotra become non-exist. This is the reason worldly life has no importance for us. We consider our community as our family. Will you be able to leave your family? Do you dare perform your own last rite? Do you think that life is like a stage in your theatre, where you can play any part that you want?" The gravity in the voice of the elder sage shook the young man.

Although he did not think the life of these sadhus to be a bed of roses but he never knew it would be so tough. In a frustrated tone he said to the girl, "Did you not study well enough about them? How will you conduct your research?"

"Do not blame your partner or whoever she is. It was your haste indeed that has brought you here or maybe the impatience of youth which thinks that it has discovered something marvellous. This is why you wander with half-baked knowledge about everything. So, tell me, can you do your own pind-daan?" It was as if the sadhu was desperate to untangle all webs in the minds of the young man.

The young man remained silent. He had no answer. Even the mere thought of performing his own last rites gave him goosebumps. Therefore, he thought it right to stay silent.

"If he passes all the tests of chanting, penance, yoga, weapons and scriptures, then a day before any royal bath during the Maha Kumbh, he is made a Naga. His head is shaved, pind-daan is performed to free him from the debt of ancestors. 'Viraj Hom Sanskar' i.e., the ritual of leaving home is conducted by the Acharya Mahamandaleshwar of the Akhara.

"Along with himself, the aspirant has to perform pind-daan of his seven generations from both the sides of both his parents and in the end his sexual organs are neutralized so that his lust is finished before he becomes a Sadhu." The old sadhu continued after he got no answer form the young man. He took a puff of the chillum and glared at him with his fiery eyes as if they would burn him.

"Mahapurush is the most extraordinary personality. He is made to take 108 dips in Ganga during the Mahakumbh and he is assigned five gurus. The aspiring Naga has got five gurus - Lord Shiva, Lord Vishnu, Goddess Shakti, the Sun God and Lord Ganesh. The practitioner is provided with rudraksh, saffron, ash and some other spiritual things which complete the apparel of a

Naga. Then it becomes necessary to rid him of all the worries and worldly attractions in this dejected state. The practitioner shaves his head and performs his own last rites under the guidance of the priest of the akhara. This last rite demonstrates that now he is dead for the outside world. The Naga will now have to follow and protect Vedic traditions and Sanatan dharma. The last stage is the most unbearable and torturous of all. This process starts with the aspiring Naga to stand under the flag of the akhara for 24 hours. He is supposed to carry a vessel full of water in his both hands and a log (a heavy object) on his shoulders. During this period the members of the akhara keep a vigil on him. Then in order to neutralize his penis, it is beaten slowly along with the help of mantras. This exercise weakens the penis gradually and brings an end to any sexual desires. Then comes the chanting of 'Om Namah Shivay', which goes on all night. All this transforms a Naga Sadhu into a warrior and protector of Sanatan dharma and the country. After he becomes a Mahapurush the process to make him a 'Avadhut' begins. To make him a Avadhut, first the thread ceremony of the sadhu who has become a Mahapurush is performed by the Acharya of the Akhara and then he takes an oath of the life of a Sanyasi."

"After the completion of this stage, the Sadhak becomes a complete Naga Sadhu. It is very difficult to enter our world and you people think our life is a joke. You live in cities, consider yourself modern and very smart but smartness does not come handy everywhere," another Sadhu, who was very tall and who had braided his hair instead of wrapping it around his head and looked scary because of his countless hanging braids, said in a loud voice. "Will you be able to give such a difficult test? Are you capable of controlling your physical and mental desires? Even now, you are roaming with a girl. You are fooling yourself and this girl as well."

"Let us go Shekhar," The girl stood up to leave but the man took her by the arms and made her sit once again.

In order to calm his curiosity, the old man said, "You will not even be able to imagine giving up your clothes. Our life is not a drama or a movie where you can act as per your wish. Our life is based only on rules, we are free creatures, but not undisciplined. You may not even know that Naga Sadhus are not allowed to wear clothes. We are only allowed to apply ash on our body and this is our adornment as well as clothing. Matted hair on the head and ash on the body…is the identity of every Naga Sadhu. We live in ashrams or temples. Or we travel on foot in the Himalayas and live in a hut in some village. Or we make a cave our home. We do not use a bed or any other means to sleep. We can sleep only on the ground, not even on a mattress.

"We garner spiritual powers through rigorous penance which we use to help and heal people."

"I am aware that Naga Sadhus possess mysterious powers."

So, can you do whatever you want to do with the help of these powers? Possessing power signifies being arrogant but you guys denounce arrogance, isn't that why you feed yourself by begging for alms?" the Shekhar spoke as if he knew everything, although he knew most of it after reading Rumi's notes.

"You fool, we acquire these powers through our penance, then how can there be any arrogance? We never use our powers for evil purposes, in fact we use them to help people with their problems. I hope you got the answers to all the questions arising in your mind.

And there is one more thing, we are the protectors of dharma, we know how to wield a weapon and annihilate the enemy as well. You will be amazed if you look into the history," said a sadhu named Gajanan almost burning with anger.

The young man was sitting stunned, but his expressions did not indicate that he wanted to return. The girl was rubbing her palms on her feet in restlessness. The regret of agreeing to her lover's quest was visible on her face.

"Come with us. You will get to know a lot more. We will tell you on the way. We cannot delay seeking alms anymore," the girl stood quickly as the middle-aged sadhu spoke.

"Wait a moment," everybody looked at the elderly sadhu as they heard his loud voice. "Gajanan, first tie your long braids and wrap them around your head. If you go out like this, people will get even more scared seeing us," he said looking at the tall Sadhu.

❑

4
Seeking Alms

They came out of the cave and started descending into the plains through cambered stairs. There was a whole contingent of sadhus who frightened even Shekhar when he got a look of them in natural light. Only ashes on their bodies, red eyes and roaring chants of Har Har Mahadev… it seemed that the sadhus walking in a queue. Barbarian is what people called them… 'he had said that without giving it a thought, but does he really want this life?' All of a sudden these questions started meandering in Shekhar's mind. 'It is his desire to seek thrill that has brought him here? Anyways Rumi too wanted to come here for her research purposes,' he consoled his mind.

Their life is not easy at all! People simply call them barbaric, but they must perform rigorous penance only through which they become Naga Sadhus. After attaining this, they devote their entire remaining life for protection and welfare of people and dharma. A deep sense of respect grew in Shekhar's heart.

"Those who make fun of Hinduism and its traditions are unaware of the depth of Hindu devotion and its customs. They don't know the extraordinary penance that the sadhus perform is beyond the imagination of common man," said a sadhu while walking towards the front.

Shekhar felt as if he had read his mind. 'Is it because of the spiritual powers that they hold?'

"Is it pre-decided where you should go to seek alms? I mean who gives alms, whom to seek alms from, isn't it all known to you by now?"

"Absolutely not," a short sadhu said who was walking side by side to the Shekhar. He must have been in his early thirties. It was evident from his conversation that he was a well-read scholar. He was fair skinned and his round face had a soothing persona which seemed radiant and confident, perhaps owing to penance.

"Even we do not know where our steps will take us. We cannot force anybody to give alms. We are allowed only one meal in a day. One sadhu is permitted to seek alms from maximum seven houses only. If he gets nothing from those seven houses then he has to remain hungry. Whatever he gets, he has to accept it with love keeping aside his likes and dislikes."

Shekhar and Rumi had to almost run to keep up with the sadhus who were walking very fast. Both of them were surprised to hear this. It is possible that they had to remain hungry for many days.

"What is your daily routine?"

"We go to sleep after eating in the evening. We wake up early before dawn during Brahma Muhurta. We take bath, do yoga, pray and this is how our day begins. After this, we do havan, 'meditation', 'vajroli', 'pranayama', 'kapal-kriya' and 'nauli-kriya'. We sleep only once a day, after having dinner in the evening."

"How are they so fit when they eat once a day and that too whatever they get?" Rumi said to Shekhar. "You go to gym, eat nutritious food and yet you are unable to walk as fast as them." Shekhar smiled when she said this laughing.

"Well, you do yoga as well, so what would you like to say about yourself?" Rumi smiled.

"Wait here. We will be back after seeking alms." A sadhu whose name was Kirat, interrupted them when a series of buildings, that were perhaps part of some habitation, came in sight. This thirty-five-year old sadhu was very lean and his bones and ribs were shining as if they were wrapped with weapons. His agility was beyond this world.

"Can't we accompany you?" Shekhar asked in amazement.

"No, and avoid asking silly questions. We do not like to talk much. It exhausts our energy." The elderly Sadhu, who everyone was calling Baba Nath, said in a straight voice and moved ahead.

Shekhar and Rumi sat on a rock. They felt an urge to rest as soon as they sat down. While their body was tired, their mind was filled with questions and those questions were making them more tired.

Shekhar took out a water bottle from his bag and handed it to Rumi and said to her, "One thing is clear that it is no joke to be a Naga Sadhu. It is only after going through an arduous test of patience and penance, one is given the title of Naga Sadhu."

"By the way, you did not have to do so much drama and you even gave them the idea that I wanted to become a Naga Sadhvi, you exaggerate so much." Rumi threw a few drops of water towards him.

"It just came out of my mouth. Maybe I was afraid..." Shekhar gave a hard laugh.

"I can't even think about becoming a Naga Sadhvi, but how did you get this idea?"

"I had seen Naga Sadhvis as well at Kumbh," Shekhar said shyly.

"You are right. Coming here opened up a whole new dimension... I feel like so many closed doors are opening. Mysteries are becoming revealed, layer after layer. So many secrets were revealed an the Kumbh Mela as well. In my view, the Kumbh is a living document of human civilization. Whoever wants to understand life should not go anywhere but come to Kumbh. There is so much to know, so much to understand and to experience. Kumbh introduces you to such seekers also who are searching the forests and mountains to find the truth and the mysteries of life and to get acquainted with it or are sitting in the most desolate places by lighting a fire after tasting the extreme materialism and understanding its futility." Rumi said while taking out a packet of sandwich from her bag. The way she said that gave a sense that she was wandering in some other world.

"Many Naga Sadhus have come from the caves or hills of Uttarakhand, Himachal Pradesh and Junagadh in Gujarat. Naga Sadhus reside in one cave for a few years and then they move on to some other caves. Therefore, it is difficult to know about their precise location. Moving from one cave to another and then another, these Naga Sadhus spend their entire life on herbs and roots and devotion of Bhole Baba. Many Nagas spend years while roaming in the jungles and they are seen in the next Kumbh or Ardha-Kumbha."

"But we also cannot deny that Akharas are the heart and soul of Kumbh and these Akharas operate through Naga Sadhus. Akharas have their own system. If you visit Kumbh and you do not learn about the Akharas then your journey is also incomplete just like us. I want to go those Akharas. You must have a lot of information about them? What is surprising is that so many highly educated people are also joining them. Take Kirat for example..."

Rumi started reading from her diary. "Juna Akhara is the largest of all Akharas at present. It is followed by Niranjani and Mahanirvani Akhara. The head of these akharas are called Shri Mahant and the chieftains are known as Acharya Mahamandalesvar. Niranjani Akhara is the most popular Akhara of all these.

"Not only this but even at the universal scale it has maximum number of educated Sadhus and Sanyasis who are the followers of Shaiva tradition and who keep long breads of hair. Kartikey is the chief deity of this Akhara who is the general of gods. Daraganj is the main centre of Niranjani Akhara. The Akharas have surrendered themselves completely to fulfil the goals for which they were established in the ancient times. To fight foreign invasion to protect lives is also a type of penance for life. However, now the primary task of akharas is religious spiritual penance only.

"And if I tell you about educated sadhus then Raja Rai who I met during the Kumbh Mela is only 27 years old. He holds a diploma in Marine Engineering from Kutch University. And not only this, 29-year-old Shambhu Giri is a management graduate from Ukraine. 18-year-old Ghanshyam Giri from Ujjain was a topper in 12th standard. He had told me that he realised about his goal after he topped the board exams. At that time, he was 16 years old and he had come to the ashram of his guru Jairam

Giri. I feel that becoming a sanyasi is the journey of becoming detached while living a life of renunciation. The main purpose and the ultimate goal of the life of Naga Sadhus is to go beyond it by intensifying the experiences of life through religious spiritual practice. Their only goal is to free themselves from external temptations and understand the depth of existence. So what do you say, are you also ready to become a Naga Sadhu?" Rumi joked while closing the diary.

Shekhar smiled and looked at her with affection. "For the moment let me take a dive in the ocean of your love, we will worry about becoming a sadhu later. But I will make a documentary on these for sure. Get up, look these Naga Sadhus are coming."

Rumi saw that the sadhu was coming towards her with alms. She said, "They have received the alms. They will not have to stay hungry."

❑

5
Ashes and Asceticism

"You can walk with us just a little longer. Then you must return. If your mind is still wandering then go to Ujjain or wherever you wish to go or you can get more knowledge from some Mahamandaleshvar of ours." The tone in which Baba Nath said this, made Shekhar and Rumi feel that there was no point in arguing or urging any more. They stood up and started walking along him.

"People believe that we indulge in asceticism only and roam around smearing ashes on our body, but in reality, we Nagas are the commandos of Dharma. We are the commandos of Sanatan Dharma. Whenever evil has befallen on Sanatan Dharma and all hopes had been lost, we entered the last battlefield for protection of Dharma. Whenever danger loomed upon the nation, whenever the culture of this nation stood on verge of destruction, whenever invaders raised their heads, we fought the battles as warriors. We have bought battle with a challenge to die for the country. We are soldiers of Dharma and have been fighting the last battle for the protection of Dharma and culture. We have fought battles as the guardians of of tradion and heritage. Actually, we are soldiers disguised as Sadhus," he said.

"Kirat, the other sadhus have gone far ahead, I will accompany them to the cave. These young people are not able to match up to our speed. I am going ahead. You stay. Maybe you could quench their curiosity."

Unknowingly, Shekhar and Rumi folded their hands in his regard. All along the way he kept taking pictures. He captured a few more pictures of him in his camera. They watched him leave for a few moments. Taking long strides, he quickly went out of sight.

"Would, you like to sit down or rather I tell you while we walk?" Kirat asked when he realized they both were out of breath.

"Let us keep walking," Shekhar was quite embarrassed. He said, "Something has been eating me up that is it the penance which the Naga Sadhu do to make their life hyperphysical. Their entire body smeared in ashes, flames of spiritual fires burning in the eyes, tripund on the forehead, trident symbolizing Shiva Shakti in the arms decked with Rudraksha and the expression of glory to Bhole on an expressionless face. Ending all ties with your family, end of all the relations and end of yourself… is this what marks the beginning of your secrets to mysticism?"

"You can say so. This is how our life begins. It is true that for Nagas their new chapter in life of Sanyas begins with the end of his earlier life. Conducting our own last rites, conducting pind-daan of fourteen generations. Our own pind-daan, pind-daan for all past present and future, all our names, gotra everything changes. Neither can we return to our homes nor can we have any acquaintances with anybody. We lose all our identity as soon as we dive in the sangam after pind-daan. It is assumed that we have no past. Parents, siblings, all our marks of life till now, the relations, we erase all these when we come out of the Sangam."

"Erasing all our identities, when we step out of the Sangam, then we are ready to walk the path of Dharma. We have one and only one purpose, protection of Dharma and chanting Har Har Mahadeva. We are supposed to go to our own house to seek the first alms."

"But why? How painful it must be for your family to see you this way? Seeking alms from them as a stranger? It must be so difficult?" Rumi was astonished. The pain in her eyes were clearly visible. "After all, which parent would want to see their child like this?"

"It must be painful for them but not for us. When there no identity left after becoming a sadhu then, where is the problem? The rule is such so that they can free themselves from all the constraints of this world. So that they can be free of their past."

"When you have given up on everything then what is the need for penance? Why take up arms? History has shown as that whenever the last efforts to protect the Dharma has gone futile, these Naga Sadhus have taken up arms and they have given and taken lives to protect the Dharma. You call yourself the soldiers who protect the dharma." Shekhar was probably struggling with some contradiction in that moment.

"We are the symbol of both scriptures and weapons. The foundation of the present form of Sanatan Dharma was laid by Adi Guru Shankaracharya. Shankaracharya was born around middle of the eighth century, when the condition and future of Indian people was not very good. Many invaders were coming here, attracted by the wealth of India. Some took that wealth back with them while some got so fascinated by the divine aura that they stayed here. General peace and order had failed completely from the incursions of the invaders. God, religion, scriptures were facing all kinds of challenges from logic, weapons and scriptures."

"Seeing all this, Shankaracharya took many steps for the establishment of Sanatan Dharma and one of which was formation of the four Peethas. These were - Govardhan Peeth, Sharda Peetha, Dwaraka Peetha and Jyotirmath Peetha. Other than this, The Adi Guru also started establishing Akharas in the form of armed section of different sects in order to counter those who robbed the temples and monasteries and those who harassed the devotees. Adi Guru Shankaracharya had begun to feel that in those times of social turmoil these problems could not be tackled by spiritual powers only. He insisted that young sadhus should strengthen their bodies by exercising and get skilled in using weapons. Therefore, such monasteries were built where such exercises or weapon handling were practiced, such monasteries came to be known as Akharas."

"In common parlance Akharas are those places where wrestlers learn the tricks of exercise. With time many other Akharas came into existence. Shankaracharya suggested the Akharas to use their prowess for the protection of monasteries, temples and the devotees. In this way these Akharas worked as a protective shield during those times of foreign invasions.

"Akhara is also a kind of monastery where the sadhus are not only imparted knowledge but they are also prepared for all kinds of battles and military customs. Naga Sadhus have an order of precedence for running the Akharas, according to which they get administrative positions like Kotwal, Bada Kotwal, Pujari, Bhandari, Kothari, Bada Kothari, Mahant and Secretary. Based on the size and importance of the Akharas, their presidents are given posts called Mahant, Shri Mahant, Jamatia Mahant, Thanapati Mahant, Mahant Digambar Shri, Mahamandleshwar and Acharya

Mahamandleshwar. Naga Sadhus are trained like a military sect and their designation is also like a military regiment. You must have seen that Naga Sadhus carry trident, sword, spear and mace with them at all times. Naga Sadhus are believed to be of two kinds—one who carry the scriptures and one who carry the weapons. Those with weapons learned to wrestle and those with scriptures got into studying the scriptures. It is the organised form of weapon bearers that is seen in the Akharas.

"In the remote areas of the Himalayas, Naga Sadhus can be seen without clothes, but when they come among the people, they wear loincloths. They always keep weapons with them and there are different groups of armed Nagas. They are known by the names of Avdhoot, Aghori, Mahant, Shamshani, Kapalik etc. Naga Sadhus get four positions which are Kutichak, Bahudak, Hans and Paramhans. It is considered extremely rare for any Naga Sadhu to get the position of Paramhans.

"The tradition of Naga Sadhus is not new, but has been going on for thousands of years. We find signs of this tradition in the coins and pictures of Mohenjodaro, where Naga Sadhus are found worshipping Lord Shiva in the form of Pashupatinath. It is said that when Alexander and his soldiers came to India, they met Naga Sadhus. Not only this, Lord Buddha and Lord Mahavir were also very impressed by the penance of Naga Sadhus and their devotion towards the motherland."

People passing by were staring at them in wonder. Although the settlement was left behind and they were on a deserted road, there were some people there. Probably tourists or people living in the village or settlement who had come out for some work.

❑

6
Kirat's Diary

"You are so young. Educated as well, how did the idea to become a Naga Sadhu pop in your mind. Did someone forced you?" Shekhar asked. Afterall what could be the reason that he became a sadhu and that too a Naga Sadhu?

Kirat stopped. "It seems your questions and curiosity has got no end, but now you will have to return and you should cover the remaining distance on your own. See, we got so indulged in chit chat that we have almost reached the cave. Jai Mahadeva!"

"Please answer Shekhar's question. It is a natural question that can come up in anybody's mind. What is your qualification?" This time Rumi asked him.

"First of all, you must know that one is never forced to become a Naga Sadhu. In fact, if one claims that he wants to become a Naga Sadhu then a thorough examination about him is conducted. Baba Nath had already told you all this. As far as my qualification is concerned, I have done a M.S.C. Once I had gone to Kumbh to do research on Naga Sadhus. I too was curious like you two. I never dreamed that I would be so influenced by them that I would leave my family, society etc. It took me a lot of time to convince the Mahamadaleshwar that I really wanted to become a part of their world. My determination was unshakable. Why did my mind push me towards this way, I have no answer for this and perhaps nobody has. Therefore, it is better to leave a few things to destiny."

"And then…"

"Your questions have no end." Kirat paced ahead.

Shekhar and Rumi stood still and watched Kirat go. Or maybe they were looking for a way out of the maze of questions and answers in which they found themselves trapped.

Just then they saw a sadhu running towards Kirat. They had heard his name on the way… it was Ratnakar. He must be fifty years old but his body was built such that it could outshine young men. Despite his naked body smeared in ashes, despite the swaying Rudraksha garlands hanging from his neck to the navel, his physique could not be hidden. Had there been no matted hair, and had there been no unkempt beard then he would appear as an avatar of the Kamadeva for sure.

He handed something to Kirat. It looked like a parcel. Kirat began to observe it. His face lit up.

"Shekhar," He came running towards them.

"Baba Nath has sent something for you. Actually, these are some notes written by me, which I had recorded in a diary when I was exploring the history of Naga Sadhus prior to their becoming Naga Sadhus. Through this you will get the information about the warrior aspect of the Naga Sadhus. When your purpose is served then hand it over to Mahamandaleshwar Girinath ji in Ujjain. May god make your journey successful and you get what you seek."

Rumi quickly took the diary from Shekhar's hand as if she had found some treasure.

"So, what do we do now?" Shekhar asked.

"What do you mean?" Rumi was engrossed flipping through the pages of the diary.

"Do you want to go to Ujjain or shall we return home?"

"Going to Ujjain will take time. It would be better to head home. Reading this diary would clear a lot of things and if I don't understand something then my guide and professor of history, Dr. Dipankar Vachaspati would be able to explain the history of Naga Sadhus and the reasons for them becoming warriors in a better way after reading this dairy."

Rumi took out the diary from her bag as soon as they got into a taxi to go to the airport. It was very thick. It had a red coloured velvet cover and the borders had fine golden lines. Har Har Mahadev was written on the first page of the diary and on the next page - 'Brajesh Tripathi.'

"It looks like Kirat's original name is Brajesh Tripathi."

"It could be so, because to become a Naga Sadhu, one has to first sacrifice his identity. All the research he had done prior to becoming a Naga Sadhu is recorded in this. Maybe he could not leave this behind, probably Baba Nath had given him permission to keep it with him. This was good, otherwise all this effort would have gone to waste. At least we could benefit from this and we would be able to understand and explain their history, difficult penance and life." There was a sparkle in Shekhar's eyes.

"Your enthusiasm is killing me." Rumi said.

"I am doing all this for you." Shekhar's eyes twinkled, and he touched Rumi's hand softly.

Rumi looked at him as if she wanted to say that she knew everything. Then she said, "general perception among the people about Naga Sadhus is quite confusing, which most people have formed by watching them roaming naked in the Kumbha mela." Rumi turned the next page of the diary and said, "in the beginning it mentions about the Akharas. Brajesh or Kirat whatever you call him, his handwriting is quite beautiful. Each letter looks like a pearl. If he wanted, he too would have taken assistance of the digital world and typed everything. By the way he had only helped us by writing this diary."

"It would take a lot of time to reach the airport. You read; it would help not to get bored till we reach the airport. Since the handwriting is so beautiful, reading it won't be a problem. You know how lazy I am in these matters. Unless I have something in front of me in a laptop, I can't read it."

Rumi got comfortable on the seat and started reading. "Akharas are not only an abode for the Naga Sadhus but it has a glorious military history. The role of Dashanami Akhara is extremely important in the military history of India. The term, Akhara gained popularity from the Mughal era. Historians believe that that history of Naga sect in India goes back to prehistoric times. Historians believe 'During the excavation of the ancient city of Mohenjodaro in the Indus Valley, the coin found there and the statue of Pashupati seated in a Digambara form and worshipped by animals on it are proof of the fact that such matted haired ascetics are also mentioned in Vedic literature.'"

"Centuries ago, Adi Shankaracharya had established the Akharas to protect the Hindu culture from the spread of Buddhism and Mughal invasions. Royal processions, decorated horses and elephants, sounds of large bells, stunts of the Naga Akharas and open display of swords and guns is the mark of Akharas. It is that group of sadhus who is master in wielding weapons. According to the sages associated with the akharas, these akharas have come in existence to explain through weapons to those who do not understand by the scriptures. These akharas have played an important role in the freedom movement as well. These Akharas had shed their military identity after independence. At the beginning there were only four Akharas, but they kept on getting divided due to ideological differences."

"According to tradition, there are a total of 13 recognised Akharas of the Shaivite, Vaishnavite and Udasin sect ascetics. These Akharas are named Niranjani Akhara, Juna Akhara, Mahanirvan Akhara, Atal Akhara, Ahwana Akhara, Anand Akhara, Panchagni Akhara, Nagpanthi Gorakhnath Akhara, Vaishnav Akhara, Udasin Panchayati Bada Akhara, Udasin Naya Akhara, Nirmal Panchayati Akhara and Nirmohi Akhara. At the head of each Akhara is the Mahant.

"Normally the word Akhara is associated with wrestling, but it is also used for wherever there is a possibility of manoeuvre. Earlier, the akharas of ashrams were called 'Beda', that is, a group of Sadhus. Earlier, the word akhara was not in use. There were pirs in the group of Sadhus. The use of the word akhara started from the Mughal period. However, according to some texts, the word 'Akhara' has originated from the word Alakh. Whereas according to some religious experts, it has been named akhara due to the arrogant nature of the Sadhus.

"It is believed that akharas were organised on military lines. Akhara have also been given the name of military regiment. The residing places of group of Nagas were known as cantonment at some point in time and military terms inspired from Islamic culture are also used in akharas. The role of Akharas has been important in the political life of North India.

"In the beginning, Naga Sadhus restricted the Akharas to spiritual activities only. They used weapons only for protection of religious sites. But later they turned into professional soldiers and evolved in an important objective in the politics of North India during the post Mughal era. They took part in all decisive battles of east and north India during the latter half of eighteenth century.

"In the eighteenth century, there were far-reaching changes in political organisations, social institutions, economic life and condition in India. The Mughal Empire declined rapidly. The Marathas' attempt to monopolize the country failed. British traders succeeded in laying the foundation of a new type of empire. Naga Sadhus not only continued to interfere in the politics of North India, but Indian kings and the East India Company also entered into agreements with them.

"In the latter half of the eighteenth century, Naga warrior Rajendra Giri emerged as the pioneer of the Gosain Naga warrior community. His early life was spent in Bundelkhand. He made his disciples proficient in the art of war by teaching them lathi, ballam, phad, akhada and wrestling and divided them into four groups on the basis of akhadas – Anand Akhada, Aman Akhada, Akhaat Akhada and Juna Akhada, which later became famous as 'Baba Sena' or 'Gosain Sena'. They..."

"We have reached airport," Shekhar interrupted Rumi. "This is all so interesting, and the way you read it, created more curosity in me. You are too good in narrating also, Rumi. This is why you win all the essay and speech competitions in college."

"Stop praising me and take out the stuff," she said, looking lovingly at Shekhar. Rumi's face turned red when Shekhar caressed her cheeks.

❑

7
Alexander's Pride is Shattered

Rumi opened the diary as soon as she boarded the flight. She was turning the pages continuously. Everything seemed so mysterious and profound to her. She was feeling sleepy, so her eyes were constantly shutting down. Although she was a student of history but it was difficult to understand the depth of facts at first instance. The history of Naga Sadhus seemed amazing to her. She had not read anything in such detail about them earlier. Like most people she also thought they were like hippies who wander around and smoke intoxicants to stay happy. She had just started to write her research paper; therefore, she was turning over the pages with curiosity. At this time, she wanted to read some very simple description or story because she was feeling tired both physically and mentally.

"Close your eyes for a while and take some rest Rumi. It is a long flight and we are tired as well. I am feeling dizzy. Read the diary when you get home. It will be with us for some time till we do not go to Ujjain." Shekhar said to Rumi caressing her hand.

"Hmm," Rumi said and rested her head on the seat and closed her eyes. The take off of the flight had been announced.

"Ma'am juice," Rumi was startled by the voice of the hostess. Perhaps she had dozed off. Even though she was feeling tired, her mind was in a turmoil. She felt a strange restlessness.

Shekhar was in deep slumber. She felt a little relaxed after drinking the juice. It is of no use to sleep, she thought. Anyways soon the hostess will start serving dinner. Rumi's eyes stuck at one place while turning the pages of the diary. The title was 'Conversation of Alexander with a Naga Sadhu.' She began to read it.

"I will establish my rule till the last corner of this world, whether my army is with me or not," swelled with pride, Alexander said to his soldiers standing before him.

His army was looking at him with amazement. 'What else did he want?' this was a question going on in their minds but they could also not abandon him.

Alexander became the king of Macedonia at only twenty years of age and since them he had harboured a dream to conquer the world. He set out with his soldiers, weapons and cavalry to fulfil his father's wish to win Asia Minor. After this Alexander got one victory after another and he started pacing towards his goal. He conquered many small and big states and reached Egypt where he established a new state called Alexandria. Here he established a new university and built many buildings.

We have conquered Turkey, Syria, Egypt and Iran and I want to conquer India, the land of prosperity and immense treasure.

"I have learned a lot about India from Herodotus and other Greek authors. Its geography and natural history fascinate me."

Alexander's Pride is Shattered

Alexander headed towards Kabul after conquering Iran, from where he crossed the Khyber Pass to come to India and reached the Indus River. Alexander conquered many small republics and made his way back towards the Indian subcontinent. The nineteen months (326 to 325 BCE) spent in battles in India were the hardest. He did not have much time to strategize for battles before he stepped into his conquest. Despite this he prepared a few strategies. Most of the states he had conquered were returned to the kings who granted his wishes. However, the entire region was divided into three parts all of which were governed by different Greek governors. As a result of Alexander's conquests, ancient Europe and India came into their first ever encounter. This had several important consequences. Alexander's invasion of India was a tremendous success. Although Greek lands in India were soon conquered by the rulers of the Maurya dynasty, who added a vast Indian province to their empire, the Greeks still had a presence in the country.

Ambhi, the Prince of Taxila and Porus who ruled in the region between Jhelum and Chenab were the two rulers of this region. Prince Ambhi surrendered as soon as he launched his attack. Alexander had to face his first and toughest resistance from Porus while he was crossing river Jhelum. Despite Alexander's win over Porus the fearlessness and courage of the Indian prince caught his eye. As a result, he returned his kingdom to him. He wanted to go east but his soldiers refused to join him. The Greek army which was tired of war and sick wanted to return home. The scorching heat in India was getting unbearable for them.

Alexander had many encounters with Naga Sadhus and every time he was left amazed. Once when he met a Naga Sadhu at the banks of river Indus, he noticed that he was sitting on a rock and looking at the sky for a long time. Alexender asked him "What are you doing?"

The Naga Sadhu answered "I am experiencing nothingness."

Before a perplexed Alexander could ask anything else, the sadhu asked him. "What are you doing?"

Alexander answered with pride and pomp "I am conquering the world. I want to go to the last end of the world but you keep sitting at just one place." Then he started laughing loudly.

Hearing his answer, the Naga Sadhu also started laughing. Alexander thought that this sadhu is a fool who is sitting in one place. The sadhu said, "There is no end in this world."

Alexander met Naga Sadhus on the banks of Indus River and was surprised to see their knowledge, philosophy and understanding of life. Plutarch, who was a Greek biographer and essayist, used the word 'Gymnosophists' for Naga Sadhus. It means 'scholar Nagas'. He wrote in one of his descriptions – 'Alexander arrested ten Nagas, who had promoted rebellion against the Greek army. These Nagas were clever and were famous for answering any kind of questions. Therefore, Alexander wanted to ask them difficult questions. Alexander put a condition that the one who gave the wrong answer would be killed immediately. The Nagas gave the right answers to all the questions. Alexander was surprised. He rewarded all the Nagas and sent them off.'

Since Alexander's army had been fighting for years and was very tired. Respecting the wishes of the soldiers, Alexander decided to return. He was looking for a wise saint, whom he wanted to take with him. Asking some people for directions, he reached a Naga Sadhu with his army. Alexander saw that the saint was meditating under a tree without clothes. He and his army started waiting for the saint to come out of meditation. As soon as the saint broke his meditation, the whole army started chanting in one voice – 'Alexander the Great! Alexander the Great!' The Naga Sadhu smiled at them.

Alexander said to him in a commanding tone "I want to take you with me while returning from India."

The sadhu answered very patiently, "You have no such thing that you can give to me. There is nothing that I do not have. I am happy with who I am, where I am. I want to live at this place. I do not wish to come with you."

Hearing this filled Alexander's army with rage that how can a simple sage dare to refuse the wish of their emperor.

'All of you calm down,' Alexander said to his men. Then he said to the sage 'I am not accustomed to hearing no. you will have to come with me.'

'You cannot decide about my life. I have decided that I will stay here which means I will stay here, you may leave.' The Naga Sadhu ordered Alexander.

Alexander was not prepared for this answer, after all he was a conqueror. He was furious. He took out his sword and put it at the neck of the Sadhu. 'Now tell me what do you choose, life or death?' Alexander asked.

'If you kill me then do not call yourself Alexander the great or whatever your soldiers call you. Because there is nothing great about you. You are the slave of my slave.'

Alexander was shocked to hear this. He is an emperor who has conquered the whole world and a monk is calling him the slave of his slave. 'What do you want to say? What do you mean by this?'

'I do not get angry until I want to. Anger is my slave. Whereas anger grips you whenever it wants. You are a slave of your anger. Maybe you have won the world, you might have defeated many warriors but you failed to conquer your anger. Therefore, you shall remain the slave of my slave.'

Alexander was astonished to hear this. He bowed his head with respect in front of the Sadhu. Alexander's pride was shattered and he returned with his army.

"Wake up Shekhar, dinner is here."

Yawning he asked, "The diary is in your hands and its pages are open. This means that you have not slept."

"I was reading a very interesting story. When Alexander came to India, he met many Naga Sadhus and each time he had a new experience. And new aspects of the learnings of those Naga Sadhus are opening up in front of me too. There are many more incidents of meeting Naga Sadhus recorded in this. I will read after having food. If you want, we can read together. Now I am not going to read it to you in the flight," Rumi joked.

"I too know a lot about Alexander. I agree that I am not a student of history like you and have a scientific attitude. Alexander came to India in 327–26 BC; perhaps like a comet and returned after showing his wonders for a total of about one and a half years (exactly nineteen months). Detailed records of his entry into India are available in Greek records, especially Arrian's 'Anabasis of Alexander', and pages after pages of Indian history books are filled with quotations from those details.

"But the truth is that he was deeply influenced by the sages, ascetics, and the wise men of India. He met many scholars in India. They told him that an ambitious person keeps trying to achieve something that is not worth the effort and when he loses everything, only his good deeds stand with him. They also kept warning Alexander against greed and excessive pride." Shekhar said and Rumi looked at him with admiration.

"I was not aware that my lover had so much knowledge about history especially about Alexander," Rumi said looking at him with affection.

"You forgot that I did a drama on Alexander," Shekhar reminded Rumi.

"Oh yes! What else can you tell me about Alexander? It will help me a lot to better understand the stories about his meetings with the sages."

"Can I first finish my dinner, if you permit?"

"While talking to you, I simply forgot that you haven't finished your dinner yet."

After drinking water, Shekhar said, "Just like Alexander wanted other foolish things in his life, he also wanted immortality. Because he wanted to conquer the whole world with his power. By that time, he had conquered half the world in a very ruthless manner and now he was getting impatient because he felt that he needed more time to complete his plan. So he was looking for immortality, for which he came to India. On the Hindukush Mountain, he met a yogi who was sitting in a deep state of meditation. People like Alexander have no discretion, so he went and disturbed the yogi's meditation.

"He asked, 'People say that in India Yogis live for thousands of years. They have attained immortality. Can you teach me immortality? In return, I can give you whatever you want.' The Yogi asked, 'What do you have?' He asked his soldiers to bring big chests filled with all the looted gems, diamonds, pearls and gold.

Opening them, he said, 'Here it is, the wealth of the whole world is here.' The Yogi laughed and said, 'You have been picking things from the soil. All these gems and gold are just soil. I don't know why you have considered it so valuable! You have not understood the value of the soil on which you walk, which gives you food every day. But a stone which you call 'diamond', which is of no use, has become very valuable. I want to explain to you that your diamonds are not valuable because you find a lot of beauty in them. There are flowers blooming everywhere which are more beautiful than any diamond. They also have fragrance and you do not notice them. But a diamond is precious, not because you see any beauty in it. In fact, diamonds are not beautiful at all. They shine and look like this because of the way they are carved. But you feel happy only because not everyone has them. This is not happiness, this is a kind of illness. This happens only because your mind has rejected death.' Hearing this, Alexander got angry.

'How dare you talk to me like that? Don't you know who am I? I am Alexander the great."

Hearing this the sage smiled and said calmly 'Had you continually, moment after moment accepted death as a process of life, your values for life would have been different.'

"Still you want to attain immortality then there is a forest, you will find a small cave in it. Enter the cave and you will find a small pond. Take few drops of water from it and drink it. You will become immortal."

He entered the cave and took the water from the pond in his hand and as he was about to drink it. Suddenly a crow sitting at the other end of the pond spoke to him, 'Hey, stop! Alexander the great fool, stop.' Alexander was surprised. The crow was not cawing but speaking Greek. He looked up. The crow said, 'Look, I drank water from this pond of immortality and I don't know since when I have been sitting here. I have been sitting here for thousands of years, I don't know what to do. Now I sit here, whatever I do I cannot die, I can't even kill myself. I have been sitting here since eternity. Do you really want this? Please think about it before you drink this water. I committed a mistake by drinking this water, you just think about it before drinking.'

Alexander stood there, shaking. He imagined he would remain on this earth after ten thousand years. What would that scene be like. He understood the point. He slowly turned back and did not drink water from the pond. He realized that death is the only thing in your life that is certain. The spiritual process begins only when you start becoming aware of your death. Alexander bowed to that sadhu and returned from there."

The air hostess served coffee and both started drinking it with great pleasure, because both of them liked coffee very much.

❑

8
Questions and Answers

Rumi fell asleep after drinking the coffee so Shekhar started reading the diary. He started from the same page which Rumi had book marked.

"I have always been impressed by Alexander, his prowess being one reason but more than that because he had experienced the wisdom of the wise men in India. He learnt a lot from the Naga Sadhus whom he had watched naked in the sun, rain and cold and eat a balanced diet, he learnt a lot from them and had his pride shattered on many occasions. Alexander was also inclined towards philosophy due to the teachings of Aristotle." Kirat had noted this down.

A picture of a Naga Sadhu was drawn on the next page. Perhaps it was drawn by Kirat! On the next page there was a picture of a Naga Sadhu with Alexander which was pasted there from the internet. His notes began again from the next page. The raging river, fort, mountain and narrow valleys on the way could not shake Alexander's courage. Shortly after entering the borders of India Alexander met a sadhu lying on a huge rock. Alexander's army was marching ahead chanting his victory. The sadhu was watching all this while he lied down. He kept on lying down even when Alexander came near him. Such a huge army marches beside someone and he still remains so calm, this all looked very weird to Alexander. He kept staring at the sadhu.

He asked the sadhu, 'Don't you feel even a little scared of me or my army? I have won the entire world. I am the master of a vast land and treasure'

The sadhu answered him in a very calm voice 'Only those who fear getting robbed of something will fear a robber. But what will you achieve by amassing such huge wealth after murdering so many innocent people?'

Alexander answered, 'I will spend my entire life with ease and comfort.'

The sadhu said, 'But I still am living my life peacefully without murdering anybody, without amassing any wealth.' The sadhu turned his face away from Alexander and closed his eyes in a calm posture. Alexander stood there watching him in astonishment. He had had his first conversation with the culture of India.

Shekhar took a deep breath. On one hand, his respect for the Naga Sadhus was increasing, on the other hand, his curiosity was surging like a fast-flowing river. Rumi had rested her head on Shekhar's shoulder while sleeping. Shekhar felt good seeing her sleeping carefree. For a moment, a smile danced on his lips thinking about that matter. On one hand, he and Rumi were planning to get married soon and on the other hand, without giving it a thought, he had told the Naga Sadhus that they had come to become Naga Sadhus and Sadhvis.

Mumbai was still around 45 minutes away. Flight was late and the pilot and air hostesses had already regrated and apologised for this. Shekhar started reading, ‘When the king of Sindh Sabbas heard about the arrival of Alexander, he decided to flee. Despite being uninterested in worldly affairs, many sadhus encouraged the king to fight the invader. Sikander got very angry when he came to know about this revolt from the Naga Sadhus and he ordered his men to capture and bring them to him. His soldiers were able to get many of them except ten wisest Sadhus. They were known to be clever and give complex yet crisp answers.’

After learning about their uncommon skill, Alexander decided to play riddles with them before taking their lives, just like a hunter plays with his prey. He did not give them any assurance of freedom; this was just a way to decide about the order of their execution.

The riddle in the proposed game had a very interesting feature in which the sadhu was ready to lose his neck if he was unable to solve the riddle. By the end another feature got added on its own which was in accordance with the Aristotelian logic. It was a deadlock similar to the liar’s paradox, in which a man says he is lying. Is he telling the truth now or is he still lying?

Greek philosopher Plutarch has given a vivid description of this game in his book ‘Life of Alexander.’ Greek philosophers and historians really had an eye and a heart for drama. In this scene too, the competition was designed in such a way that the questions and answers were put in a complex format of infinite clauses and direct and indirect speech. Alexander said that everyone would be asked a question and whoever gave the wrong answer would be punished with death. To ensure fairness, he made the oldest monk the judge of the competition. Then began a clever and fascinating competition between strength and wisdom, life and death.

Questions and Answers

Alexander to the first sadhu - Which if more in number in your opinion, the dead or the alive ones?

First sadhu - Alive because the dead are no longer in existence.

Alexander to the second sadhu - In your opinion who produces bigger animals earth or water?

Second sadhu - Earth produces everything as oceans also are a part of earth.

Alexander to the third sadhu - Which is the cleverest animal?

Third sadhu - Man has not yet discovered about this.

Alexander to the fourth sadhu - Why did you encourage Sabbas, the king of Sindh for revolt?

Fourth sadhu - Because I wanted him to either die with dignity or live gracefully.

Alexander to the fifth sadhu - Which is greater? Day or Night?

Fifth sadhu - One day, day before one day.

Alexander to the sixth sadhu - How can a man become most loved?

Sixth sadhu - If he is powerful yet inspires no fear.

Alexander to the seventh sadhu - How can one become a god instead of man?

Seventh sadhu - By doing something which no man can.

Alexander to the eighth sadhu - Which is more powerful?

Eighth sadhu - Life, because it supports many evils.

Alexander to the ninth sadhu - How long is right for a man to live?

Ninth sadhu - Till he does not consider death better than life.

After hearing all the answers Alexander turned towards the tenth sadhu who he asked to act as a judge. He wanted to know about his decision that which among the nine answers was the worst. Being the wisest, the sadhu said that each was worse than the preceding one. Alexander smiled and answered that all the sadhus including the judge should be executed.

Then the sadhu reminded him about the initial conditions of the game that the sadhu giving the wrong answer would be killed not the sadhu giving the worse answer. The judge argued further that no answer could not be both correct (as accepted by Alexander) and the worst (final answer) at the same time without explaining that not only his but all the answers before him were correct. There was no condition about the quality of their answers.

During the game a sadhu said laughingly, 'Abnormal questions require abnormal answers.'

Finally, he set them free and honoured them with expensive gifts. He also asked the sadhus if they wanted more to which he cleverly asked him for immortality. Alexander got very sad upon hearing this unusual request and he replied in despair that he has no such power as he himself was a mortal.

Then a sadhu asked him, 'Why do fight wars, why do you ransack cities and countries and what is the need to kill so many people? When one day you must leave all your wealth and land for someone else.' Alexander answered patiently, 'It is the wish of God that motivates him to do such things, just like tides can't happen without wind and trees can't sway without gust of air, similarly humans can't make a move without the wish of God. I did not want to fight battles but the hunger to become a conqueror of the world prevented me from that.'

Then the sadhu said, 'So many people were ruined because of your invasions. It is also true that many people became prosperous because of your invasions. Those who robbed others properties had to hand over them to other people ultimately and nothing remained permanently with anybody.' Alexander returned after hearing this.

Rumi was awake. "How long before the flight lands?" She asked yawning.

"Ten minutes. Only two pages remain to complete Alexander's story. I was thinking of reading them in the meantime. I can't wait till morning."

Rumi smiled. "I knew you won't be able to stop yourself once you start reading it. In any case, this dairy will remain with me so read as much as you can now."

Shekhar began reading further, 'There is one more story about Alexander and a wise Sadhu. He saw an unusual looking sadhu under a tree at the edge of the jungle. The almost naked man had long hair, tangled locks, unkempt beard and wore only a loincloth. Alexander observed him for several days without disturbing him. The sadhu would sit in a certain posture under the tree for hours and keep looking at the horizon. One day he asked the Sadhu, 'I see you every day sitting under the tree in a particular posture for hours and looking at the horizon. What are you really doing?'

Sadhu did not reply. Alexander said 'We are preparing for the war, putting in so much effort and you are just sitting here and doing nothing. What is all this after all?'

Sadhu did not reply.

Struggling hard to keep his anger in check, Alexander asked the sadhu once again ‘at least tell me about your purpose in life. You are only wasting time by sitting here.’

This time, the wise sadhu looked above and asked a counter question ‘What is your purpose in life?’

‘I am Alexander and am on my way to conquer the world.’

‘What do you plan to do after that?’ the sadhu asked with curiosity

‘I will take all the wealth, horses and elephants from the conquered lands to Greece.’

‘Let us assume you accomplish your goal emperor, what comes after that?’

‘I will take all the men of these evil countries as my slaves and all the women to establish my dominion in Greece.’

‘What an idea! All the men as slaves and women as entertainers!’ the sadhu remarked sarcastically. ‘Suppose you achieve that objective too, what will you do after that?’

‘After that, I will undoubtedly sit on my throne and relax.’

‘That is exactly what I am doing,’ the sadhu said with a smile.

The sadhu was not frightened even after seeing the armed soldiers, he was not scared of their aggressive nature. Seeing the worried lines on his forehead, the sadhu said in a calm voice, ‘Why did you need to conquer and kill so many people, when only six feet of land is needed after death.’

Alexander was so impressed that he said he wanted to take one of the sages with him to Greece. All refused to go with him except one. This sage was later named Kalanos by the Greeks. However, he was also known by other names such as Kalyanaswami, Shobhanaswami, Sphinx and Kalyan. He was a disciple of Dandamis, an Indian teacher and gymnosophist. Alexander sent his messenger Onesicritos to bring Dandamis from Taxila.

'Hail to you, O teacher of the Brahmins!' said Onesicritos, after having sought out Dandamis in his forest retreat. 'Alexander the Great has called you. I have come to fetch you. If you obey him, he will bestow you with precious gifts, otherwise he will cut off your head!'

The sadhu said 'Alexander is no god, he too shall taste death. How can such people be the master of the world when he has still not seated himself on the throne of inner universal dominion? Neither has he yet penetrated the netherworld nor does he know the path of the sun through the central regions of the earth, while the nations living on its borders have not even heard his name! If Alexander's present dominion is not sufficient for his desires, let him cross the river Ganges; there he will find a territory capable of sustaining all his people. Know that all that Alexander gives and the gifts he promises are utterly useless to me; the things I value and find real use and value in are these leaves which are my home, these blooming plants which provide me with daily food and the water which is my drink; while all other possessions which are eagerly gathered prove disastrous to the gatherers and only cause misery and vexation, from which every poor person suffers to the fullest. As for me, I lie down on the leaves of the forest and need no protection. I close my eyes in quiet slumber; for I have nothing to guard against, that would make sleep disappear. The earth provides me with everything. I go wherever I please and there is no care with which I trouble myself. Who is Alexander to cut off my head, he cannot destroy even my soul.'

'Let Alexander scare those people with such threats who desire wealth and who are afraid of death because both these weapons are equally powerless. We sadhus are not afraid of death. So go and tell Alexander that Dundamis does not require any of your things and hence he will not come to you and if there is something you require from Dandamis then you should come to him.'

Alexander takes Kalanos, a true yogi, with him to Greece as his Guru. On a certain day, in Susa, Persia, Kalanos gave up his aged body by entering a funeral pyre in front of the entire Macedonian army. Before leaving, Kalanos embraced all his close companions, but said only this much to Alexander, 'I will meet you soon in Babylon.'

Alexander left Persia, and a year later died in Babylon.

The flight landing was announced. Rumi and Shekhar started packing their luggage.

❑

9
History Scholar Professor Vachaspati

It was 1:00 am by the time they got out of the airport. "Shall I drop you to home?" Shekhar asked Rumi putting her bag in the cab.

"No, no, it won't be a problem, I will go. You also go home and take some rest. I have go to meet professor Vachaspati tomorrow evening. If you want you can come there. I will read the remaining thing written in the diary with him so that the events of history can get proper clarification."

"I will come. Besides, the moth always follows the flame," he smiled mischievously. "I will come directly from the office."

"It is not right for someone who desires to become a Naga Sadhu to be in a romantic mood all the time boy! Learn to control yourself." Rumi laughed and got into her cab.

Shekhar felt embarrassed, but what could he do! After all he is madly in love with Rumi.

Rumi had booked an appointment with Prof Vachaspati on phone in the morning itself and messaged Shekhar. He too wanted to meet her because she had already told him about their meeting with the Naga Sadhus on phone. He had laughed very hard hearing about Shekhar's idea of them becoming Naga Sadhu and Sadhvi.

"Shekhar is very naughty Rumi, but beware, his antics should not land you in trouble. Keep a tight rein on him."

"Surely, I will do sir." Professor Vachaspati did not joke very often so Rumi did not let this opportunity to joke get away.

Professor Vachaspati not only taught history but was a scholar as well. He had studied so many subjects in depth. Rumi was pursuing her PhD under his guidance and he was very impressed by her dedication and intelligence. He was fifty but walked so fast that even the young would struggle to keep pace with him. Brown kurta made of Khadi and white pant cut pyjama was his dress code. He was so fair that would make the Kamadeva blush. Golden frame on his round face suited him quite well. He was almost bald and therefore the shine on his head dazzled the eyes in sun. God knows if the shine was natural or if he used some special oil. That shine was visible on his face as well. He used to wear gold rings on the middle finger of both hands. He would often say, 'This is my style.'

His wife Deepshikha taught philosophy and cotton saris were her dress code. She was not fair like Prof. Vachaspati, but she had a golden complexion. She was of a serious nature, but she used to meet the professor's students who came to their home with great love and left no stone unturned in their hospitality.

When she went to his house in the evening, he listened in detail to everything she said and asked whether the fatigue of the journey had gone away or not. Prof. Vachaspati, sitting with Rumi in his study, kept turning the pages of the diary for a long time. Meanwhile, his eyes brightened many times and different expressions appeared on his face. Meanwhile, Shekhar had also arrived.

"Shekhar you spoke nonsense to those Naga Sadhus and had to face their anger, but Rumi you managed to bring an invaluable treasure with you. It seems I will also get to learn a lot more. This is how a disciple should be, why Shekhar, what do have to say to this?"

Shekhar felt embarrassed hearing this but spoke as soon as he heard applause for Rumi, "You are absolutely right sir. I too am a fan of Rumi's wisdom. This is why I follow her wherever she commands me to. She had landed me among the Naga Sadhus and that too in a cave. I could not think of anything at that time seeing Naga Sadhus in front of me so I blabbered whatever came to my mind. How could I tell them that my girlfriend is doing research on them. Who knows that might have flared their anger even more," Shekhar said laughing.

"Sir, let's talk about what is written in this diary, and not me!" Rumi said.

Meanwhile, Deepshikha ji had sent tea and snacks to the study. Rumi knows that when the professor is in his study or with his students, Deepshikha ji never comes and disturbs him. It was as if there was an unspoken agreement between them that they can certainly give advice to each other, but will not interfere in each other's work. Rumi had been visiting Prof. Vachaspati's house for a long time, so she knew that there is a lovely relationship between them and she wants the same relationship with Shekhar. She considered Prof. Vachaspati her ideal.

Her eyes suddenly turned towards Shekhar, who was looking at the books kept in Professor Sir's library. He also asked her through his eyes what the matter was, to which Rumi shook her head in no. Rumi likes it when Shekhar takes care of her. She feels very safe with him.

"By the way I today I want you meet someone else as well. She will be here in a little while." Professor Vachaspati said and Rumi looked at him with curious eyes.

"You must remember that last year I went to San Francisco for a conference. There I met Dr. Michael Peterson. He introduced me to his student Roselina. She has keen interest in Indian culture, history, monks and ascetics. She had come to India a couple of years ago and had met some sadhus as well. Now I don't know if she has met any Naga Sadhu or not but if she went to Allahabad then she must have met them. I hope she has some information which could be useful for your research paper."

"Wow, this is very good," Shekhar said before Rumi could say anything. "In the meantime, I will tell you what I have read," Prof. Vachaspati said, sliding his glasses up his nose. This is probably his way of starting a conversation. "Akharas have been mentioned at many places in the diary and we also know that Mahanirvani Akhara is the third largest Akhara among the Akharas established based on Vedic Hindu traditions. It is a Shaiva Akhara. Kapil Muni is the chief among the revered sadhus of this Akhara. He is also considered to be the one who started the Naga tradition. It is the oldest among the Akharas, it is said that this Akhara was already established. Adi Shankaracharya had reorganized it during his lifetime. This Akhara is responsible for the worship of Mahakaleshwar Jyotirlinga. The head of this Akhara is known by the title of Acharya Mahamandleshwar. Once selected, the sadhus remain on this post for life. The five main sadhus of the Akhara are also called Pancheshwar, who are selected in every Kumbh. In 1260, under the leadership of Mahant Bhagwanandgiri of Shripanchayat Mahanirvan Akhara, 22 thousand Naga Sadhus liberated the temple located in Haridwar Kankhal from the occupation of the army of the invading Slave Dynasty after a fierce battle. After this, in 1774, to protect the Kashi Vishwanath temple, they fought fiercely with Aurangzeb's generals and emerged victorious. In 1771, the Naga ascetics of the Akhara also strongly opposed Aurangzeb's attempts to capture Garhkuntha.

"The history of Shri Panchayati Mahanirvan Akhara is very glorious, and the context of the establishment of the Akhara is also very interesting. It is said that Shambhu Giri Maharaj, Shankar Giri Maharaj, Parshuram Giri Maharaj, Mahadev Puri, Ramgiri, Bali Ram Giri, Kapil Sevak Giri Maharaj once went together to Nepal for rigorous penance. During the Nepal trip, they met an unknown Mahatma on the way. Impressed by the purpose, sacrifice, penance and knowledge of the Mahants, he blessed them and gave them two sticks to save their lives. These two sticks later turned into spears. These two spears named Surya Prakash and Bhairav Prakash are still enhancing the beauty of the Akhara and every Vijayadashami they are worshipped with full rituals. Bhairav Prakash and Surya Prakash spears in the form of gods move ahead of the procession of Akharas during Kumbh Mela and these gods in the form of spears are first given a bath in the Ganga during the royal baths in Kumbh. After that, Acharya Mahamandaleshwar of the Akharas, Shri Mahant of Mahamandaleshwar Jamaat and other Naga Sadhus take bath. Shri Mahant Ravindra Puri Maharaj, Secretary of Shri Panchayati Mahanirvani Akhara says, 'On the day of Dussehra, we worship our ancient gods and weapons, because Adi Jagadguru Shankaracharya established the tradition of scriptures and weapons to protect the nation. Weapons are also present in the hands of our gods and goddesses.'

"So, I was talking about the Nepal journey. There they worshiped Lord Pasupathi. In their dream they got an order to please Kapil Muni Maharaj through their penance. There they met a boy who might have been of about 15 years after crossing the Ganga, so they took him along with them. All the Mahants unanimously named him Devdutt Giri.

"After three years of penance in Gangasagar, Lord Kapil Muni appeared before him and ordered him to establish his own Akhara. It is said that the very next day an Akashvani (voice from the sky) said that Devadatta Giri is the youngest, he should be called Chotiya and he will establish the Akhara. The headquarters of Mahanirvani Akhara is in Daraganj Prayagraj. And..." Prof. Vachaspati stopped while saying this. Seeing the young woman coming in through the door, he said happily, "Hey Roselina, I was waiting for you."

Roselina was very tall. She must have been around five feet nine inches tall. Her fair complexion and red cheeks looked like Kashmiri apples. She was wearing a long maroon coloured dress which had small yellow flowers. She was wearing shoes which she was about to take off when Prof. Vachaspati signalled her to keep them on. Her brown eyes were small and her golden hair gave her a doll like look.

She smiled and folded her hands in greeting to the professor and sat on the chair placed next to him. Her smile was very sweet and friendly.

"I was also very keen to meet you Professor. Michael Sir, often talks about you." She said in a very composed tone. There was a sweetness in her voice which easily attracted people. Then she said smiling, "I must say your wife is really sweet. She greeted me very warmly. I met her outside and she told me that you are in the study."

Hearing this, Prof. Vachaspati beamed as if he was being praised.

"Thank you. Rumi-Shekhar, this is Roselina. Roselina, Rumi is doing research on Naga Sadhus under my guidance. I hope you both have similar interests so you will be able to help each other."

"Oh that's great. Nice to meet both of you." Roselina said while shaking hands with them.

Rumi and Shekhar had not thought that Roselina could speak such clear Hindi. Her pronunciation was also excellent, although English words were used occasionally, perhaps it would be easier for her to speak the difficult words in English. Anyway, Rumi and he used a lot of English words along with Hindi.

"During my stay in Allahabad, I also met some Naga Sadhus. Before that I did not know anything about them, as prior to that I had met only common sadhus and ascetics. But the lifestyle of Naga Sadhus and their covering their entire body with only ash created a curiosity in me to know about them. Whatever I know, I would definitely like to share it," she said smiling.

"Roselina, we were talking about Akharas. You know about it, you told me over the phone."

By then tea and snacks had arrived again. Prof. Vachaspati extended the plate of samosas towards Roselina and she picked up the samosa saying, "Wow, I love samosa."

Thinking that they will start after eating, everyone started enjoying tea comfortably. Meanwhile, Prof. Vachaspati showed the diary to Roselina and started telling how Rumi and Shekhar got this diary.

❑

10
Role of the Akharas

Roselina said, "I met Shri Mahant Dharm Das of Nirvani Ani Akhara. Initially he kept on refusing to meet, but agreed on repeated requests. He told me that 'it was made a rule for young sadhus living in monasteries and temples that they strengthen their bodies through work out and attain proficiency in some sort of weapons as well. For this, such monasteries were established, where along with exercise, training in using weapons was also given. These monasteries came to be known as Akharas. Akharas were established for the protection of Sanatan culture and Dharma. There are different rules, regulations and traditions for different akharas associated with different sects of Hindu Dharma. Sadhus involved with these akharas are called Nagas. Naga means one who stands by his words, one who sacrifices his life for the protection of his country and its people, one who forgets his family and relatives and serves, worships God and protects the country. Whenever crisis looms over the society and there is a threat on religion then these sadhus of the akharas along with worship, pick up arms and fight for the country and society.

"As far as I know, it was Ved Vyasa started the organised form of forest dwelling hermits for the first time. After him,

Shukdev and then many sages and saints gave a new shape to this tradition in their own way. Later, Shankaracharya established four monasteries and formed the Dashnami sect. Later, the tradition of Akharas started. The first Akhara 'Akhand Awahan Akhara' was formed in 547 AD.

"The role of Dashnami Akharas is very important in the military history of India. The foremost among the Dashnami Akharas is Mahanirvani Akhara, whose headquarters are located in Daraganj, Allahabad. The names of many brave and valiant warrior monks of this Akhara such as Rajendra Giri, Anup Giri alias Himmat Bahadur, Mahant Mukund Giri of Jhabua, Daulatpuri of Jodhpur, Bhairavpuri of Jaisalmer and Neelkanth Giri of Udaipur are recorded in history,"

"It is believed that akharas were organised on military lines. They have also been given the name of military regiment. The residing place of Naga Sadhus were also called continents in early times. Akharas have played an important role in the political journey of northern India. We get a glimpse of political activities of Naga Sadhus in northern India from twelfth century to the first half of eighteenth century. Prior to this Naga Sadhus had a reputation of being scary and unruly.

"But their task was to protect the religion, how did they get involved in politics? They even protected so many kings. Isn't it weird to know that some sadhus were politically active?" Rumi asked.

"You are right, but in the beginning, Naga Sadhu were involved only in religious activities. They picked up arms only for the protection of religious sites. But in view of the need of time, they also came into the role of professional soldiers and emerged as the 'sadhus who played an important role' in the politics in post Mughal era. Interestingly, is that they took part in all the decisive battles of Eastern and Northern India during the later eighteenth century. At that time the Nagas used to be disciplined and well-armed. They were the best cavalry and infantry."

"There were strange notions about the Naga Sadhus. I have seen a photograph of Naga soldier, which was made by an officer of the East India Company, James Skinner in the early nineteenth century," said professor Vachaspati while taking a thick book out of his bookshelf. He showed that photograph in the book. The picture depicted a man who was naked from head to toe and who had a leather belt strapped on his waist from which a dagger and a bag of gun powder hung. He had matted hair and they were locked in a big bun, just like a protective helmet. He held a long barrel army gun in his left hand and had a vermilion tilak on his forehead.

He said, "They kept weapons and gunpowder in these bags. Nagas had a special reputation as raid and close combat hand to hand soldiers. Under the leadership of Anup Giri they developed into a full-fledged infantry and cavalry force, comparable to the best armies."

"Tell us something about the heroics of Anup Giri, Roselina. Earlier you had also mentioned him as a valiant warrior," Shekhar said. His interest was getting rising continuously. Rumi was busy making notes. The way Roselina was telling the tale of Naga Sadhus like a story, it seemed like she is watching a movie.

"Sure, I will tell that, but first I want to tell you about the situation during the eighteenth century so that you can understand the importance of his role. It is written in detail in this book. By the way I read on google that Anup Giri's guru Rajendra Giri had also played an important part in battle. It is also said that Anup Giri Gosain was an ascetic, a man devoted to the Hindu god Shiva, a Naga Sadhu who was one of the most revered holy personalities of India. According to William R. Pinch, author and historian of 'Warrior Ascetics and Indian Empires', Anup Giri Gosain was a warrior ascetic. Of course, the reputation of Naga Sadhus was 'fearsome and unruly'. The obvious difference is that the Nagas of the 18th century were extremely well armed and disciplined and were said to be excellent horsemen and infantry soldiers."

Roselina went silent for a few moments because her eyes were still stuck at the picture. It looked as if that photograph had impressed her a lot. "It is a beautiful picture." She picked up the glass of water, took a sip, fixed her hair with her hand and leaned back on the chair and read the book and said, "There were far fetching changes in the political organisations, social institutions, economic life and conditions on India during the eighteenth century. The Mughal empire which had given the country a sense of unity and had led it towards progressive developments in various fields, was on a steep downfall. The Maratha failed in their attempts to take control of the country and the British merchants were successful in laying the foundation of new kind of empire. With the decline of Mughal empire, many regional powers emerged out of which some were independent while some were dominions. Bengal, Awadh, Hyderabad and Maratha were some of such powers.

"Many weak rulers ascended to the throne after the death of Mughal emperor, Aurangzeb. Muhammad Shah was also one of them, during whose reign two important states of Mughal empire - Bengal and Awadh got independence. After the death of

Muhammad Shah, Ahmed Shah came to power and he appointed Safdarjung as his minister. Awadh is the same independent state whose nawab, Safdarjung is given the credit to give shelter to Naga warriors and bring them to the battlefield during the Mughal era. Naga warriors were the best warriors in the army of Awadh.

"In the late half of eighteenth century, Naga warrior Rajendra Giri Gosain emerged as the pioneer of the Naga community. He trained his disciples in lathi, ballam, far, akharas and wrestling and made them proficient in the art of war. Impressed by Rajendra Giri's bravery, some kings endorsed the establishment of his akhara near their forts and entrusted him with the responsibility of their security, while some kings made him the fort commander.

"By the time Mughal emperor Ahmed Shah ascended the throne, the process of disintegration of the Mughal Empire had reached its peak. During the time of Ahmed Shah, a leader of eunuchs named Javed Khan had gained a lot of influence in the court and the emperor had become a puppet in his hands. He plotted against minister Safdarjung as well. Then Safdarjung redirected his focus towards his state Awadh.

"The state of Awadh shared its border with Ruhelkhand and it was controlled by Ruhelas and Bangash Afghans. Safdarjung wanted to weaken the powers of Afghans living in the neighbourhood of Awadh. He provoked Kayam Khan, who was ruling over Farrukhabad, to attack the Ruhelas. Kayam Khan was killed. Safdarjung established his control over Bangash region.

"Afghans spread in the regions of Awadh. Only the Allahabad province remained different form this. Along with marching towards Awadh Shadi Khan, the step brother of Ahmad Shah Bangash marched towards Allahabad with twenty thousand cavalry and infantry. In the meantime, Ahmad Shah camped in Jhusi situated one mile east from the fort of Allahabad and he also set up his artillery on the fort built on the mound of King Harbong and started firing. The siege of Allahabad continued from February 1751 to April 1751 and the Afghans did not get the success that they were expecting. The main reason for this was Bakaulla Khan who was a great warrior, getting amazing assistance in the form of Rajendra Giri Gosain. Rajendra Giri had camped in Allahabad with his disciples during the Magh mela. When Rajendra Giri noticed the residents of forts surrounded in danger, he selflessly along with his companion Nagas attacked the Afghans. He killed many Afghans.

"The battle took a new turn with the entry of Naga Sadhus. A historian has written 'A very brave Naga Sadhu along with his disciples used to reside just beside the fort of Allahabad at the banks of Ganga, who spent his time in the devotion Mahadeva. He was very upset with the destruction caused by the Afghans and got ready to assist Bakaulla Khan without any invitation, but he declined to the request to move inside the fort and camped at few distance away from the fort with his disciples. Every day he assembled brave soldiers, rode on beautiful horses and attacked Afghan camps and did not return without killing a handful of bold soldiers from the enemy camp. He continued to slaughter the enemies till the siege continued.' Thus, every attempt of the Afghans to capture the fort of Allahabad was thwarted by the courageous resistance of the Naga Sadhus.

"Rajendra Giri Gosain had the honour of becoming the pioneer of Naga warrior Sadhus. He was beyond the attachment of life and death. His disciple Anup Giri and his younger brother Umrao Giri became his successors after his death and carried forward his traditions and the command of operation of Naga army came in their hands." Roselina said returning the book to professor. "I would definitely like to read this book professor."

"Pinch has written many more astonishing things and facts in his book," said Professor Vachaspati, moving his glasses.

The three looked at him curiously.

"The astonishing army of Naga Sadhus had a good reputation in hand-to-hand combat. Under Anup Giri they developed into a full-fledged infantry and cavalry that could compete with the best. In the late 1700s, Anup Giri and his brother Umrao Giri commanded over 20,000 men. By the end of the 18th century, the number of ascetic soldiers wielding arms increased dramatically.

"Thomas Brooke, a judge of Varanasi, formerly called Banaras, also wrote, 'Anup Giri was omnipresent, because he was a man everyone needed. He was condemned because he was like a man who, while crossing a river, kept his feet in two boats and was ready to leave the boat that was sinking.'

"Not only this, Anup Giri fought battles on all fronts. In the battle of Panipat in 1761, they fought for the Mughal Emperor and Afghans against the Marathas. Three years later they were present with the Mughal army against the British in the Battle of Buxar. Anup Giri has also played an important role in the rise of the brave Greek, Najaf Khan in Delhi. Later he turned away from the Marathas and sided with the British. In 1803, in the last years of his life he enabled the defeat of Marathas against the British, an event that placed the East India Company in the most powerful position in South Asia."

Before Professor Vachaspati could say anything else, Deepshikha's voice came from the door. She came inside and said, "Professor sir, I know that you don't feel hunger or thirst because of work, but please be kind to these people. It is 10 o'clock at night. They must be feeling hungry. Dinner is ready. Come out and then let them go home. Discuss the rest tomorrow," she said while giving a mocking scolding to the professor.

"As you command my queen!" Said Professor Vachaspati with his head bowed down. Deepshikha laughed.

Rumi, Shekhar and Roselina too could not supress their laugh.

❑

11
Abdali's Invasions

When Rumi reached Prof. Vachaspati's home next evening, neither he nor Deepshikha ji was at home. Both had to leave suddenly for some work. But they had instructed Ramdeen Kaka, who worked at their house to make everyone who came sit in the study.

In that solitude Rumi began to read Kirat's diary that she had left with Prof. Vachaspati. There was something written in red ink at one page and some words were underlined as well, so Rumi started reading that, 'Guru Dattatreya was the guru of Nagas. Guru Dattatreya is assumed to be a part (ansh) of Lord Shiva. According to Matha tradition, Dattatreya Deva is associated with the Dashnami sect, which was organised by Adi Shankaracharya under the four Mathas. Apart from the Mathas, he also organised a group of warrior sadhus for the protection of Sanatan Dharma. Later they came to be known as Naga Sadhus, who did not fear death and batten, trident and swords are their weapons. They also keep musical instruments, conch and other weapons with them.'

Roselina had also mentioned about this. Kirat also must have written about Anup Giri in this, thinking this she started to turn the pages very attentively. One instance had a mention about

Rajendra Giri, 'He was considered to be an immortal (mrityunjay) warrior and Safdarjung had so much respect for him that he never refused to anything he said. Regarding him, there were orders that the royal drum of Deewan should be played on horses (this honour was bestowed only to highest ranking Mughal Mansabdar) and instead of saluting Safdurjung, he used to bless him like a Mahant. It was popular among the people that he was a magician and swords and canons had no effect on him.'

"Hello Rumi, you have already reached. I am totally impressed with your passion. Where is your boyfriend? You are both madly in love with each other, right?" Roselina asked frankly while sitting on the chair.

"He will come straight from the office. He will probably be late," Rumi said shyly. Seeing the expressions of Rumi and Shekhar, the previous day, Roselina understood that they loved each other.

"So should we start with Anup Giri today?" Rumi asked changing the topic.

"Oh yes, I remember, yesterday the conversation ended with him. Like I told you yesterday, after Rajendra Giri, the command of operation of Naga army was given to him and his brother. I had prepared some notes, let me read them to you. After the death of Safdarjung, Anup Giri and his brother Umrao Giri devoted their services to his brother Shuja-ud-Daula. They both remained an important power in the politics of the later Mughal era from 1753 to 1804. In their fifty-year long political life, these warriors participated in many wars on behalf of Nawab Shuja-ud-Daula of Awadh, Asaf-ud-Daula, Jawahar Singh Jat, Najaf Khan, Raghunath Rao, Mahadji Scindia, and displayed unprecedented bravery. Impressed by the bravery of Anup Giri, Shuja-ud-Daula awarded him the title of 'Himmat Bahadur' and the estate of Sikandra and Bindki.

An important event in the early days of Shuja-ud-Daula's rule was the assistance provided by the Nagas to Shuja against Balwant Singh, the Raja of Banaras. During the time when Safdarjung was caught up in civil war in Delhi, taking advantage of his absence, the jagirdars (landlords) of Awadh strengthened their position. During that period, Balwant Singh greatly expanded his power. When Shuja marched towards Banaras, Balwant Singh's army stood firmly against him at a place called Pandura. At this time, to avoid unnecessary bloodshed and to prevent further delay in his journey, it was deemed appropriate to negotiate a compromise and Anup Giri was appointed for this task. Demonstrating his diplomatic skills, Anup Giri set the terms of the agreement in a way that was acceptable to both parties.

The assistance provided by the Nagas to the king of Banaras, Balwant Singh against Shuja during the early days of reign of Shuja-ud-Daula is also an important event. When Safdarjung was struggling with civil war in Delhi, the feudalists of Awadh took advantage of his absence and made their position quite strong. During that period, the king of Banaras, Balwant Singh, massively expanded his power. When Shuja set off towards Balwant Singh's army, they fought bravely at a place called Pandura on the way. At this time, to prevent unnecessary bloodshed and to not postpone his journey for a long time, it was considered appropriate to make a compromise and Anup Giri was appointed for this task. Anup Giri, showing his political acumen, fixed the terms of the compromise in such a way that both the parties accepted it."

"Sorry we had to go somewhere. But looking at you two it seems you are excha nging information at a very fast rate."

Prof Vachaspati said taking off his jacket. "By the way, I have another good news for you Rumi. This morning, historian Dr Sudip Deshmukh had come to the university. He stays in Ahmedabad but he is in Delhi for a seminar. I have invited him to dinner today. His intellectual thinking is amazing therefore it is always pleasant to listen to him. If you both wish, you can record his conversation because he speaks so fast that it is impossible to note it down."

Hearing this both Rumi and Roselina looked at each other beaming about the exciting news. By that time Shekhar had also arrived. Otherwise, Rumi was worried that he might not be able to meet Prof Deshmukh.

"You guys continue your conversation, I will go and help Deepshikha and come back. This is how it is. Shekhar especially you should understand this very seriously otherwise keep getting scolded by your wife for your entire life."

"Don't take him too seriously, Shekhar." Amidst there humour they did not notice when Deepshikha had come to the study.

"You come out, today I will definitely make you help." She laughed and they both walked towards the kitchen.

Roselina began to read the notes, 'In 1757, Anup Giri helped Shuja-ud-Daula against the princes of Delhi. By the end of 1756, Ahmed Shah Abdali, the emperor of Afghanistan once again came to India. Afghan ruler Ahmed Shah Abdali became the ruler of Afghanistan and founder of Durrani Empire after the death of Nadir Shah in 1748. He attacked India several times from 1748 to 1758 and continued plundering valuable wealth and shedding blood with his army. At that time Mughals were very weak and there was no other Hindu power in North India to oppose the Islamic invaders. He made his biggest attack on Delhi in January

1757. At that time Alamgir II was the ruler of Delhi. He was a weak and cowardly ruler. He made a humiliating treaty with Abdali, in which one condition was to give permission to loot Delhi. Ahmed Shah stayed in Delhi for a month and kept looting. He amassed great wealth in this time.

'Abdali's greed increased after looting Delhi. He also planned to plunder the Jat kingdoms of small states around Delhi. To gain control over Braj, he took full advantage of the condition of feud between the Jaats and the Marathas. From Delhi, Ahmad Shah Abdali marched with his army of Pathans towards Agra. The first encounter between Abdali's army and the Jaats took place at Ballabhgarh. There Jaat leader Balu Singh and the eldest son of Surajmal, Jawahar Singh tried to stop the huge army of Abdali with his small battalion of his men. He fought valiantly but had to face defeat against the enemy.

'Abdali's fierce plunder of Mathura and Braj, where he had a conflict with the Naga Sadhus was very cruel and horrific. Abdali reached Mathura on 15th March 1757 and crossed river Yamuna to set up his camp at Mahavan, ten kilometres south east of Mathura. Gokul was located around three and half kilometres from Mathura. It was the place of Naga Sadhus where four thousand Naga Sadhus were present. Ahmad Shah Abdali had given orders to massacre and burn down all the cities in between Agra and Mathura. Ahmed Shah sent his twenty thousand men under the leadership of two sardars to plunder Mathura. He ordered them 'My brave warriors! Mathura is a sacred place for the Hindus. Raze it down completely. There should be no building visible till Agra. Wherever you reach, kill and plunder. Whatever one fetches in the loot shall belong to him only. All the soldiers should cut the heads of the infidels and put them before of the tent of the chief sardar. For every head, a reward of 5 rupees will be given from the royal treasury.'

Roselina could not read any further. "It was ghastly and cruel. Numerous Naga Sadhus were killed. Indian history is rather brutal."

"You are right, and yet Indian history and culture pulls you back to India again and again."

Suddenly Rumi, Shekhar and Roselina noticed that another person was standing beside Prof Vachaspati.

"Meet Dr Sudeep Deshmukh. His fame is not only spread across India but the entire world," said Prof Vachaspati, introducing him to everyone.

"Vachaspati Sir, don't make me look so big. I am a junior to you in both age and knowledge," said Dr Deshmukh bowing his head in front of him.

Rumi, Shekhar and Roselina were all amazed to see the humility and modesty of such a great historian. He must have been around 45 years of age, had a normal height. He had a long face and a slightly plump body. His hair was thick and completely black. He had a thin moustache and he was wearing a T - shirt and jeans. He had rings on both the hands, which he was twirling while talking. 'Every person is unique,' Rumi thought. 'But he is so humble and simple that no one can even imagine that he would be sharing his views on various aspects of Indian history in India and abroad. It is true that a laden tree remains bent.' Rumi's heart was filled with respect for him.

"Right Dr Deshmukh, the more I read about the Indian history the more impressive it becomes. I am honoured to have this opportunity to meet you," Roselina said while greeting him with folded hands.

"I am elated as well as proud to know that you put our culture in such high regards," Dr Deshmukh also replied to her greeting with folded hands.

"You must know about Abdali's invasion of Mathura and Gokul, please tell us more." When Shekhar requested, he looked at him deeply, took the last sip of coffee, placed the cup on the table and said, "It was a very cruel act by Abdali. Most of the people are unaware of the sacrifices laid down by Naga Sadhus because till date it is the Afghans who have been glorified more than them. A fierce battle took place between sadhus and Afghans. When Ahmad Shah reached Gokul, Naga Sadhus were waiting to face the cruel Afghan army with tongs in their hands. When Abdali saw this, he ridiculed them and took the sadhus lightly. Naga Sadhus were aware of the acts of Abdali and that is why they stood upto teach Ahmad Shah Abdali a lesson.

"A few moments later the atmosphere of that place went quiet and perhaps it was giving an indication of a massive storm that was coming. Suddenly the chants of Har Har Mahadeva started echoing in very loud voice. Naga Sadhus, with tongs and tridents in their hands and a resolve to defeat the Afghan army, launched an assault on the Afghan army. Witnessing his soldiers being torn to pieces, Abdali realised that these sadhus have entered the battlefield as Mahakaal himself for the pride of their land. The tongs and tridents proved so deadly in front of huge canons and swords that the Afghan army was scattered and retreated miles behind the battlefield.

"There was bloodbath in Mathura and the entire city was filled with corpses. The heads of Sanyasis and vairagis were cut off from their bodies. It is said that in that battle the Naga Sadhus were carrying swords in one hand and the scriptures in the other. They had to save the religion as well as the country. Had the Afghan army managed to march further, uncountable people would have been massacred, Hindu temples would have been destroyed, but every sadhu demonstrated his valour and before dying each sadhu had killed hundreds of enemies. Two thousand Sadhus, who stood like a rock in front of swords and canons with tongs and tridents had attained martyrdom in that battle. But the most important thing was that the enemy army could not move ahead a step. They were killed where they were standing or they got scared and retreated. Although two thousand Naga Sadhus were martyred in this fierce battle yet ruthless Abdali had to run away from the battlefield. The bodies of Abdali's men were scattered everywhere. This scene swept the ground from beneath the feet of Abdali and he somehow managed to flee. Coincidentally, an epidemic gripped the city and many Afghan soldiers died due to this and Ahmad Shah Abdali was forced to retreat.

"Thus, Gokul was saved from plunder due to the valour of the Nagas and due to divine intervention. Abdali once again ransacked Vrindavan while returning from Gokul-Mahavan. Abdali had amassed around 12 crore rupees from the loot of Mathura - Vrindavan alone, which he took with himself on thirty thousand horses, mules and camels."

"Dr Deshmukh, is it true that Abdali had rained such havoc in between Delhi and Mathura that there was no such hut left in the Agra - Delhi Road which had even one living soul in it?" Roselina asked him. It was as if all this was hard for her to believe.

"Yes, this is the heart wrenching truth," said Dr Deshmukh in a very serious tone. His eyes were filled with tears as if he was paying a silent tribute to the Naga Sadhus in his mind. "But this is also true that Ahmad Shah Abdali was so terrified after seeing this fury of the Naga Sadhus that whenever he spotted a Naga Sadhu, he used to flee that place. Or we can also say that whenever a foreign jihadi invader comes to know that Naga Sadhus are taking part in a battle, instead of fighting they run away from the battlefield."

Along with Roselina, Rumi also started looking at Dr. Deshmukh in dismay after hearing his words. Pain was also visible on his face.

Many layers of history were yet to be uncovered.

❑

12

The Sacrifices that are not Recorded on Paper

Rumi's mind was disturbed when she left from Dr Vachaspati's house after dinner. The account of the event at Gokul and the sacrifices of the Naga Sadhus were playing in her mind like a movie. "What a tragedy it is Shekhar that historians have only sung praises for heartless and plunderers like Taimur, Akbar and Babar whereas the warriors who sacrificed their lives to protect the honour and pride of the country have been erased from the pages of history. It is a misfortune for us that we know nothing about these brave warriors of India who have sacrificed themselves for the country and religion on every step. History books do not even mention them. They remain naked and that is what people pay attention to and that too with a view of mocking them," Shekhar could sense the tremble hidden in Rumi's voice.

He held her hands. They were going for a walk, just a few yards.

"Actually, it is indeed unfortunate Rumi. About the Naga Sadhus, most people in India only know that they remain in samadhi all the time or that they are intoxicated with cannabis at all times, but that is not at all true. They do not know that the history of Naga Sadhus who are smeared in ashes and dressed only in a loincloth has been that of warriors. Naga Sadhus are the real example of bravery and faith who inspire us to protect our motherland and culture against foreign invasions. It is the brave history and long tradition of Naga Sadhus which is not influenced by the materialistic desires," Shekhar said in a very philosophical manner. In the past few days, he had learned a lot about the Naga Sadhus.

"The interesting thing Shekhar is that our historians may not have given them due importance but Megasthenes, the Greek ambassador in the court of Chandra Gupta Maurya, accounted the presence of Naga Sadhus as, 'A philosophical sect of Brahmans or Naga Sadhus who lead an independent life and refrain from meat or cooked food and lived only on fruits. They spend their entire lives almost naked in the belief that God has given us a body to cover the soul. It is their belief that God is light, but not like sun or fire, that we can see with our eyes, but by god they mean scriptures through which the wise recognise the deeper secrets of life. They take the name of gods with utmost respect and worship them through mantras. There are no women or children with them. They live their life naked. In winter they live under the open sky in the sun, but in summer when the sun becomes very hot, they live in grasslands and under trees in humid places."

"I am happy that you are working on Naga Sadhus. At least the paper that you will write will tell the young generation about their sacrifices and bravery. Every person in India today should know about how Naga Sadhus have left their Samadhi and Sanyas and have shown twice the bravery of any warrior against their enemies for the country."

"And I am happy that a student of science who is an engineer is taking interest of history of India," Rumi said teasing Shekhar, trying to break the seriousness of the atmosphere.

"This man can do anything for you, but don't forget that I am also associated with theatre and it is due to that that I have to dig into history many times. But it seems tonight you are not going to get any sleep.

"Why? I am feeling sleeping already," Rumi asked in amazement.

"Because you have brought Kirat's diary with you today from Prof Vachaspati, " Shekhar said looking at the diary that Rumi was holding in her hands.

"May be," she laughed. "But first drop me home."

"As you wish my queen!" Shekhar said and started booking a cab from his phone.

Shekhar was right when he said that Rumi would not sleep. Despite her eyelids being heavy with sleep, she opened Kirat's diary thinking that she would read a page or two. When she saw a part written in green colour in the diary, Rumi started reading it. It was clear that Kirat used to write some important parts in ink of different colours. Perhaps with the intention of making separate notes or to remember them, perhaps.

"Maha Kumbh is held in four cities of India, Haridwar, Ujjain, Nasik and Allahabad, hence the process of becoming a Naga Sadhu also takes place in these four cities. Naga Sadhus also have different names, so that the place from which they have taken initiation may be identified. For example, those who take initiation in the Maha Kumbh of Prayagraj are known as 'Naga', those who take initiation in Ujjain are known as 'Khooni Naga', those who take initiation in Haridwar are known as 'Barfani' and those who take initiation in Nasik are known as 'Khichdi Naga'. The responsibility of protecting the flag of religion lies on these Naga ascetics.

"There is a Kotwal in every Akhara. This Kotwal acts as a link between the Naga Sadhus and the Akharas. After completion of initiation, when the sadhus leave the Akhara and go to the jungles or caves to do Sadhana, then this Kotwal conveys the information of the Akharas to them. In the Mahaparvas like Simhastha, Kumbh and Ardh Kumbh, these people reach on the information of the Kotwal.

'At present, new aspirants are initiated into becoming Naga Sadhus at the Kumbh Mela only. Out of the 13 Akharas, initiation into becoming Naga Sadhus is given only in Shaivite Akharas. Among these, the maximum number of Naga Sadhus are initiated in Juna Akhara. During the Kumbh Mela, Naga Sadhus are the first ones to take a royal bath. Only after them can anyone else enter the holy river for a royal bath.'

There were some pink coloured pages in the diary, perhaps they were pasted separately. The title on the first page was written—'My experiences'. Rumi understood that it must contain the details of his meeting with the Naga Sadhus. Kirat had written in a very lyrical way about what happened during the Kumbh Mela in Allahabad. She started reading each word very carefully – 'The fog that had covered the Sangam city has cleared. The aura of the golden rays of the sun is adding radiance to the liveliness of the camps of the Akharas. The hustle and bustle of devotees, energized by the warm sunshine of the rising sun of Magh, has started on the main road of Sector 4 of the Kumbh city. On seeing a group of sadhus outside the Sri Panch Awahan Akhara on the left side of the road, the feet automatically stop. There are many other people who have already stopped. Everyone's eyes are on this group.

'Amid the strangeness of the Akharas and the grandeur of the saints, their charm is different. Strange attire, unique style. A brass snake crown on the head, a figure of a snake with its hood raised on it in the front and a peacock feather on a cylindrical pillar at the back. Two round metal rings hanging from the ears through threads, wearing dhoti-kurta and saffron shawl on the body. Immersed in singing away from the world. The sweet sound of the bell on the handle of a stick tied with fibrous cloth. I was mesmerized. Meanwhile, a voice came from the side - these are the Jangam Sadhus. They have come from Kurukshetra only to beg for alms. They will knock at the door of the Naga Sadhus. Jangam sadhu means such sadhus who take donations only from the Mahatmas. It is believed that these sadhus originated from the thigh of Lord Shiva.

'The group of singing and dancing sadhus enter the Akhara premises. Curiosity tempts me to follow them. The most powerful Akhara of Maha Kumbh, has a row of huts on the left and right. Every sadhu has his Ishta (deity) in his hut and a burning Dhuni (fire place) in front of him. What is this? I saw that the head of the Naga Sadhu, who was sitting motionless till now, started swaying on its own. The songs of the Jangam sadhus have a great impact on his Dhuni. The Nagas are pleased. They take out something. The stick with the bell of the Jangam sadhu moves forward. It touches the alms that are received.

'Strange scene, who blessed whom, who was pleased, it was not easy to understand. Jangams move ahead, I also followed them. It is 11 o'clock. I did not realize how an hour has passed. Jangam sadhus are busy pleasing other Naga sanyasis. Heads are shaking, sticks are moving, bells are ringing. Curiosity creates more commotion inside. This right around Nagas? As soon as I come out of Juna Akhara, I stop the sadhu who looks to be the oldest in the group. I am a little hesitant and so is he. He tells his name as Puran Jangam. In the conversation, the story comes up that being the priest of Dashnami Naga Sadhus, he has the right to take alms from Naga Sadhus. I remember my priest. He also considers himself to have rights over us. He tells – we are householder Sadhus. The lineage tradition of Dashnam resonates in our songs. The secret of the happiness of Naga Sadhus is now out in the open, but the desire to know the mythological reference has become stronger.

'Quenching my curiosity, he said – it has been mentioned in Shiv Purana that during the wedding of God Shiva, Brahma and Vishnu requested him to take some offerings. Bholenath declined this request and produced a sadhu from his thighs (Jangha) and they came to be known as Jangam. Jangam completed the wedding ceremony by taking offerings from Brahma, Vishnu and singing songs. I bow to him and move ahead. There is a story behind every tradition in Maha Kumbh. I move towards Niranjani Akhara. I am sure that the bells of Jangam sadhus will be ringing there too.

'I come to meet sadhu Narottam Giri, he explained the importance of Guru in Sanyas and recited a chaupaayi from Ramcharitmanas - Raghurai went to his Guru's home to study, he gained all knowledge in a short time (गुरु गृह पढ़न गए रघुराई, अल्पकाल सब विद्या पाई). Even at that time, King Ramchandraji had left his parents and spent five-six years with Guru and Lord Krishnaji too had stayed with Guruji and received education along with Sudama.

'When I asked him about becoming a Sadhu, he said, it is not easy to become a Sadhu. For this, one has to renounce wealth and material things, respect and disrespect, this is the Guru-disciple tradition, for which one needs to renounce first. Sanyas initiation is taken only after renouncing everything. First of all, ego has to be renounced, the disciple who comes with curiosity, he gets Sanyas initiation quickly. When any calamity befalls Sanatan Dharma, the Naga group comes forward. Rudraksha is our adornment, the same Rudraksha is our deity, which is the adornment of our Lord Shiva.'

Rumi fell asleep while reading, but even in her dreams she kept seeing Naga Sadhus holding tongs.

When she woke up in the morning, it was nine o'clock. Her mother was muttering angrily, "What is this? There is no fixed time to sleep or wake up, nor to eat or drink. Get married soon and then do whatever you want. Let Shekhar take care of you. I cannot tolerate your tantrums. I don't know where you roam around hanging your bag. What would we have done if something had happened to you in that deserted place among those Sadhus? I don't know what kind of subject you are researching? Enough of studying, now settle down."

"Oh Ma! You have started again. You will be the one who will weep the most after my marriage," Rumi said hugging her mother,

"If the daily drama of mother and daughter is over then please give me the breakfast, Mrs Kirit Dave." Whenever father used to tease mother, he used to call her like this.

"You are the one on leave today but I will get late for office," Manohar Dave said smiling, "And my dear, how is your research going? Work hard and earn fame."

"Yes, Papa. Prof. Vachaspati has introduced me to Roselina and Prof. Deshmukh. I am getting to know a lot and Kirat's diary is an eye opener. I must finish the work and return the diary to Ujjain. he has given me this diary with so much trust, it is my duty to return it to him in safe hands."

"It should definitely be returned, after all it is Kirat's precious treasure. When your research is over, do go to Ujjain to return it."

"We can discuss the rest of the things over breakfast. You don't say her anything so she does whatever she wants," said her mother while serving breakfast and Rumi and Papa started eating breakfast quietly.

❑

13
War against the Mughals

In the afternoon, Rumi sat down to read a novel by Shivani which she had brought from the library so that the storm brewing in her mind could calm down a bit. Also, Shivani was her favourite author. Ahmad Shah Abdali's brutality and bloodbath was troubling her mind since last night. When her mother came in the room for something, seeing her lost in thoughts she sat beside her. She was on leave today. Rumi knew that no matter how much her mother scolds her, but she never ceases from encouraging her.

"What is troubling you so much? Your research work is going well. Prof Vachaspati is an excellent guide. Is there any confusion about Naga Sadhus troubling your mind? Truth is that due to a few sadhus and babas indulged in unethical activities, our society views the guardians of Dharma also with suspicion. But everybody is not the same."

"Ma, after meeting the Naga Sadhus I have no doubt about them in my mind, but I regret that they have been sacrificing their life for the protection of Dharma from the very beginning, and the common people are unaware of them. In fact, they do not hesitate from talking rubbish about them when they see their naked form in the Kumbha Mela. It is not easy to tolerate cold, rain, heat, wind with only ash smeared on your body, but people mock this guise of theirs. They are even called as Aghoris. People do not even know that there is a difference between Aghoris and Nagas," Rumi looked at her mother to check her reaction, if she was getting bored or not.

"Our society is still a salve of hearsay, beta. Just because of this, nobody tries to find the truth or dig the facts. Only researchers and historians try to explore the facts and our rich past. Even I know that Aghoris possess some powers of black magic, whereas the Nagas are as warrior monks and they are forever ready to wrestle physically or mentally.

"Aghoris are the devotees of Bhagwan Shiva and Devi Kali. They live in a mystical aura and follow a strange lifestyle. Aghoris do not worship idols. They indulge in marijuana and alcohol to concentrate. Like Nagas, Aghoris seek transcendence and enlightenment. They believe that the use of drugs and alcohol take them to that dimension which brings them closer to God. Aghoris believe that absolute darkness is something that take them towards self-realization or enlightenment.

"Although Hinduism is entirely different from this thought, but this philosophy seems to work for the Aghoris. Hindus believe in multiple gods and worship them with full devotion. Aghoris believe that there is only one supreme being – Bhagwan Shiva. According to Aghoris, the other gods in which Hindus believe are just the manifestation of Shiva. Bhairav is that form of Shiva which is related to death.

"Most of the Aghoris like to live with the dead in the crematorium, because their rituals are primarily associated with dead bodies. They live life in solitude and therefore they live in such places where people do not go very often. Living in isolation helps them stay away from society and perform their rituals without any interference.

"In order to become a Sadhu, the Aghoris also go through a very arduous process, just like Naga Sadhus. Naga Sadhus have to give their test of penance in an akhara whereas Aghoris give their test of penance in the crematorium."

"Wow! Ma, you never show but you too harbour lot of information. Come on tell me some more. You are a teacher of social science, you too read a lot."

"I do not know a lot but I can tell you that we Hindus have faced a lot of atrocities at the hands of the Mughals and their acts of invasion and tyranny are mentioned in our textbooks in a way as if they were heroic deeds. We read about their atrocities but the kind of sacrifices made by Sadhus, saints, teachers and scholars for the protection of Hindu culture find no mention in them. The Mughals were extremely atrocious. Like the British, they too looted our country but the massacres carried out by them is also not less. The honour of women was in danger during the time of the Mughals."

"I am going to write about all this in my paper," the anger in Rumi's voice was evident.

"In the sixteenth century, the Naga Sadhus were reorganised by the great Adwait Acharya Madhusudan Saraswati in Bengal in order to protect the Hindus from the Mughals. Madhusudan Saraswati was a philosopher of Adwaita Vedant tradition and contemporary of Akbar. His name is etched in golden letters in many histories of his pioneering service to spread Sanatan philosophy, cultural rejuvenation and most importantly, igniting a blazing fire of unity among the Hindu community. In a country that was reeling under the continuous barbarity of Muslim invasions, Madhusudan Saraswati reached Akbar's court in Agra and complained to him about the attacks on sadhus by the Muslims. When his complaint was not addressed, he reorganized the Naga Sadhus and they took action to protect the Hindus from the atrocities committed by the Muslims. William R. Pinch has described its historical basis in his book 'Soldier Monks and Militant Sadhus'. Despite the debate on whether this theory is true or not, there is evidence that after Madhusudan Saraswati returned from Agra, the Naga Sadhus assembled in Varanasi and took an oath to protect the Hindus. The system he laid the foundation of later came to be known as the Akhara system of Sadhus and Sannyasis."

"Mughals have harmed both India's people as well as religion. May be this is why the era of Mughal rule during medieval India is considered to be a dark chapter," Rumi said suddenly as if she recalled something.

"The sad part is that it was the practice of the Mughals to launch unprovoked attacks against Sadhus, sanyasis and saints even in peace time. The aim behind this was to gradually weaken the larger Sanatan society by harassing or killing these Sadhus. Distressed by this, but without fear, Madhusudan Saraswati decided to put an end to the collective fanaticism. So, he went to Akbar's court and said, 'Our sanyasis are repeatedly suffering the twin blows of maleccha rule and intolerance of Muslim fakirs. If you want your name not to be tarnished, protect our sanyasis from them. Or allow us to make some arrangements for our own protection.'"

"So, did Akbar extend the hand of assistance Ma?"

Rumi was listening to her mom with a lot of interest.

"No, so Madhusudan Saraswati decided to take matters into his own hands. It was as if he had sounded the bugle to protect Sanatan Samaj and called upon people to join. People of any caste were free to join his new initiative to protect Sanatan Dharma. Thousands of Hindu warriors of all castes were initiated into Sannyas and a new system was born with the clear objective of protecting the ancient, timeless and original religion of this land.

"When Madhusudan Saraswati returned from Agra after meeting Akbar, the Naga ascetics organized a massive conference in Varanasi to lend their support to him. A carefully hidden fact of the history of the Naga Sadhus is that they were the first armed protectors of Hindu pilgrims to Varanasi against the invading Muslim barbarians. This is the main reason why the Naga Sadhus hold such a respected position and earn reverence to this day at festivals like the Kumbh Mela. They are the original front-line warriors, protecting the Sanatan society and Dharma, dying for it, dying in its service. At that time, it was named the Sanyasi Movement."

"I had read that the French traveller Tavernier wrote that in the early seventeenth century there were about twelve lakh sannyasis and eight lakh fakirs in India," Rumi said and again looked at Mother. The way she was describing it, it seemed as if she could feel the reality of it. Perhaps because of the passion to know or understand something, which had taken root in her about the Naga Sadhus.

"In fact, the Sannyasi movement which began in 1770 and continued unabated for several decades was not an accident. It was completely coherent and was merely the continuation of a long tradition. This is why the activities of the Sannyasis and

Fakirs continued without any interruption till the beginning of the nineteenth century. Thereafter the British introduced a series of highly repressive measures to control them. As a result, the confrontational nature of the Sannyasi groups lost its edge. However, the religious and spiritual activities of the Naga Sadhus and Aghoris continued unabated in the decades to come. Now even in the twenty-first century all the Akharas of North India have a considerable number of followers," Rumi continued.

"Kirat has written in his diary that in his book Anand Math, Bankim Chandra Chattopadhyay has painted the Sanyasis as the selfless residents of a sacred monastery. Historians say that the monks who revolted against the British in 1760 were Dashnami Naga sanyasis, who wore little or no clothes and lived in akharas and these akharas or monasteries also served as armouries and training centres."

Seeing Rumi's eyelids getting heavy while talking, her mother came out of the room. She thought it would be better for her to sleep at this time. She knew that she had been reading till late.

Rumi fell asleep but even in her dreams she could watch the scenes of the battle playing right in front of her eyes, about which she had read in Kirat's diary. Kirat had written that Naga Sadhus had fought many small battles which no one knows about. Naga Sadhus had also saved the Khatu Shyam temple by fighting against the Mughals.

"We Mughals have played Holi in blood in different provinces of India, now we will march towards Jaipur and Jodhpur. The kings of these provinces have a lot of wealth and property and the grandeur of the temples is also amazing. My soldiers, march forward fearlessly, we have to crush India beneath our feet," said

Murtaza Ali Khan, the governor of Emperor Shah Alam II riding on a horse, encouraging his fifty thousand soldiers.

The spirits of the soldiers were high with incessant victories. It was year 1779. "We will march towards Jaipur through Shekhawati. We have already plundered Sri Madhopur, my brave men. Now we shall plunder and ransack the temple of Khatu Shyamji."

"Stay where you are and retreat. Otherwise, none of your soldiers shall live." Murtaza Ali Khan was startled when he heard the roar of so many voices.

Leaving their samadhi and meditation, many Naga Sadhus stood in front of him with tridents and swords in their hands, with fire burning in their eyes. They were being led by Saint Dadudayal Mangaldas Maharaj, the founder of Dadu Pant, known as Kabar in Rajasthan. We are certainly less in numbers but we can fight twice as tough as you. We know very well how to deal with invaders like you.

"We can do anything to protect our Dhundar region and Khatu Shyam temple. You won't be able to do anything." Hearing the roaring voice of Sant Dadudayalji, Subedar Murtaza Ali Khan pulled his elephant back for a moment but then his roaring laughter echoed in the very next moment.

"A beggar and naked sage like you can cause no harm to me. My army of fifty thousand men will trample you in a moment. Why are you desperate to embrace death? Let us do our job and we shall leave." Subedar Murtaza Ali Khan's arrogance was emanating from his words and gestures. His army was looking at him with a sense of pride and was waiting for his orders to attack.

"Anyways you are already frightened, that is why you have brought the Nathavat, Kutchawat and Shekhawat along with you. Even when put together you cannot fight the Mughal army. Charge!"

A fierce battle started. Naga Sadhus were beheading the Mughal army with their tridents and swords. Each Naga Sadhu was overpowering ten soldiers. The army was not able to move forward and suddenly Subedar Murtaza Ali Khan treacherously attacked Saint Dadudayal Mangaldas Maharaj from behind. His head fell but despite losing his head he kept wielding his sword like a fierce warrior. Seven battalions of Dadupanthis were attacking the Mughal army from all sides. Dressed in loincloths, wielding five weapons like trident, sword, spear, arrow and dagger, these Naga Sadhus kept on fighting.

"Kill them, cut these sadhus into pieces! Look in front of you Chuhar Singh Nathavat of Dungri is coming towards you with his two sons. My brave men, attack!" Murtaza Khan shouted but before anything could happen, Chuhar Singh and his sons beheaded many soldiers at once. Their own bodies were full of wounds and eventually they too were martyred in the battle.

The land had become quite slippery due to the blood flowing from the dead bodies of the Mughal soldiers and because of that the legs of Naga Sadhus fighting on foot were slipping and sinking continuously on the ground. But that did not deter their morale.

"March ahead! Even if we have to give our lives, but we will not let these infidels reach anywhere near the temple." voices of Dalel Singh of Sewa, Saledi Singh Shekhawat of Dujod, Hanuwant Singh of Balara, Bakht Singh Khud and Surajmal Bisau, Nrisinhdas Nawalgarh and Amar Singh Danta arose from all sides.

They too were martyred one after another fighting with the armaments of the Mughal soldiers. Apart from Kayamkhani

Mishri Khan, Kayastha Arjun and Bheem, Swaroop Badwa, Mahadan Charan, Mauji Rana also sacrificed their lives to save the Khatu Shyam temple. But before that all these brave hearts killed Murtaza Khan along with his elephant. When they saw this, the Mughal army fled.

"Sant Maharaj!" all the Naga Sadhus assembled around him saying this.

"Careful with his lifeless body," said a weeping Naga Sadhu. His dreadlock was unlocked and long strands of hair that were wet by his tears, were swinging across his cheeks.

"Take him to the Khatu Shyam temple. Maharaj ji has laid his life to protect it," the swarm of Naga Sadhus was gushing towards the temple like a flood.

They were chanting "Sant Maharaj ki Jai, Sant Maharaj ki Jai."

"We were able to save our temple but could no save him from those evil Mughals. If only someone could have saved Sant Maharaj!" their grieved voices rung aloud.

"Save him from the Mughals, someone please save him." Rumi was shouting in her sleep. She was shaking vigorously.

When she woke up, she saw that her mother was trying to wake her up.

"Rumi, wake up. It seems you had a bad dream. How many times I have told you not to get so possessive for something that it overwhelms your mind and body."

Rumi could not understand that the blood she had seen flowing in her dreams just now, did that happen to sadhus for real?

❑

14
Protecting the Vishawanath Temple

"You stay at home today," said Manohar Dave when he returned home in the evening and learnt from Kirti, how Rumi had gotten scared in her sleep.

"But Papa, everybody will wait for me at Prof Vachaspati's house and every day is precious. Roselina and Dr Deshmukh had said that they will talk about the Vishwanath temple in Kashi. Naga Sadhus have played an important role in saving it. Kirat has also written in detail about this in his diary. It is important for me to go," Rumi began walking towards her room to change.

"I understand that, but it is not good to put so much pressure on your mind. Let's watch a movie today. It has been a long time since we watched a good movie," said Manohar Dave trying to persuade her.

"Oh, believe me papa, even if I go to watch the movie with you, I won't be able to enjoy it. You and Ma go, I am leaving."

"She won't listen to anybody until her research is complete. But to tell you the truth, I enjoyed a lot having the discussion with Rumi," Kirti said smiling.

"Thankfully, now my daughter won't have to face your wrath. Let us watch the movie. We shall go to Prof Vachaspati's house while returning and pick up Rumi."

When Rumi reached Prof Vachaspati's house, she saw that everybody was already there and were waiting for her. Even Shekhar was there. She felt embarrassed.

"Sorry, I'm late," she said as she sat in the chair. She took out the phone from her bag, and saw there were five missed calls from Shekhar. His eyes questioned, if everything was alright to which she signalled with her eyes that everything was good. But Shekhar could see very clearly the tiredness and a strange restlessness on Rumi's face.

Rumi took out Kirat's diary from her bag and kept it on the table.

"So, did you read anything else Rumi?" Roselina asked with curiosity.

"Yes," Rumi gave a short reply. She did not want to discuss Khatu Shyam Mandir at that time. She was still haunted by that horrific event.

"Anything interesting?" Roselina asked her again.

"Will talk about that later, let us hear Dr Deshmukh today and I believe you too have brought your notes with you," Rumi changed the topic.

Shekhar looked at her again. Rumi's behaviour did not seem normal to him today. But he did not think it right to asked her about this in front of everyone.

"Today I am going to tell you about the barbarity of Aurangzeb. Mughals had always targeted the Hindu temples to fulfil their greed. From time to time, Mughal invaders had attacked religious infrastructures and Sadhus. Whoever ascended the throne, displayed their cruelty and those who came in the guise of plunderers, they too did not hesitate in raining havoc. But whenever this happened, Naga Sadhus revolted by forming Akharas to fight under one umbrella. They became a formidable force and waved saffron flags symbolizing the Hindu Vedic tradition. Naga Sadhus were trained to fight against the anti - Vedic invaders. This is the reason the Hindus still respect Naga Sadhus even today and consider them a representative of the god," Dr Deshmukh started his talk. In the meantime, he was continuously playing with his ring. Today he was dressed in a blue colour safari suit and his personality was shining even more in it.

Deepshikha ji was not at home, so Prof Vachaspati rose up twice to give some instructions to the house help.

"Let us do away with dinner tonight please. Ma'am is also not at home. We can't trouble you every day," Roselina said to which Prof Vachaspati replied "No trouble, it is my pleasure."

Rumi knows that he won't listen to anybody so she said, "I will also help you in the kitchen, Sir."

"You should sit down; I will be back in a minute. Don't waste your time," Prof Vachaspati's voice sounded like an order.

"Yes Rumi, I will not be able to stay till late today. I have to catch a flight for New York at 1 a.m. I have come only for you. I will share whatever information I have," Dr. Deshmukh said this time, turning his rings vigorously. He was going to go straight to the airport from here. "The past of Kashi Vishwanath temple is very sad, it can be said, because it was demolished many times and it was constructed many times. But the best part is that today it stands proudly and the new generation is witnessing its splendour. The past was sad, but if the present is pleasant then it helps in healing the wounds a little," he became emotional.

'It is indeed thrilling for historians and archaeologists to come face to face with the past of buildings, on one hand it is also painful,' thought Rumi.

"It is believed that the city of Kashi situated beside Ganga is located on the tip of the trident of lord Shiva, it is one of the 12 jyotirlingas where Kashi Vishwanath is seated. This city of Kashi, situated like a bow on the banks of the purifying Bhagirathi Ganga, is truly a purifier of sins. Lord Shankar loves this place very much, so he gave it his capital and his name and Kashi's Nath is Kashi Vishwanath. Kashi Vishwanath temple is one of the 12 Jyotirlingas and is at least as old as the Mahabharata era," said Roselina.

"Mughal rulers tried to destroy the Vishwanath temple many times. Qutub-ud-din Aibak was the first to desecrate it in 1194 AD. He was then a general under the army of Mohammed Gauri. The destroyed ruins remained neglected for some years. Like other temples, this temple was also rebuilt. It was rebuilt from the middle of the thirteenth century under the patronage of a Gujarati merchant. Then Kashi was again plundered by the Sharqi rulers of the Jaunpur Sultanate and then by the Muslim army of Sikander Lodhi in the fifteenth century after which Raja Todarmal rebuilt it in the latter part of the sixteenth century i.e. in 1585.

"According to Chinese traveller Huen Tsang, there were hundred temples in India at that time. But Muslim invaders demolished all the temples and built mosques on them. The Vishwanath temple which was renovated by King Harishchandra in the eleventh century before Christ was built by Emperor Vikramaditya. Muhammad Ghori destroyed this temple after looting it in 1194. It was built but in 1447 it was ransacked once again by the Sultan of Jaunpur, Sultan Mahmud Shah. Once again, a grand temple was built at this place in 1585 AD by Pandit Narayan Bhatt with the help of Raja Todarmal."

"I have heard that the unarmed priests of this temple were also attacked once during the reign of Aurangzeb and at that time the chief priest had jumped into the well carrying the Shivalinga with him. The priest died and the Shivalinga was left in the well itself. Aurangzeb built the Gyan Vapi mosque at the place of temple," Roselina said.

"You have heard it right," Dr Deshmukh said in a serious tone. He sat on the chair resting his back as if he was in deep pensive mode. All the eyes were looking towards him. He picked up the glass of water and drank it all. It was as if he was trying to control some sort of anger brewing inside him. He spoke again, "Shah Jahan passed an order in year 1632 and sent his army to demolish this magnificent temple. The army could not demolish the central temple of the Vishwanath temple because of the strong resistance from the Hindus but they managed to demolish 63 other temples.

"Historian L P Sharma has written in his book, Medieval India 'On 18th April 1669, Aurangzeb passed a royal decree to demolish the Kashi Vishwanath Temple. This decree is still preserved in Asiatic Library in Kolkata. This demolition is recorded in 'Masid-i-Alamgiri' written by contemporary author, Mustaid Khan. On Aurangzeb's order, the Gyan Vapi mosque was built in place of this temple. On 2nd September 1669, Aurangzeb was informed about the completion of demolition work of this temple.

'Not only this, in 1669 all the subedars and musahibs were ordered to demolish all the Hindu temples and schools. A separate department was initiated for this. There was no way that all the schools and temples of Hindus could be demolished, but Keshavdeva Temple of Mathura, the Somnath temple of Patan and almost all the big temples, especially the temples of North India were demolished at this time.'

"Some other historians have also written facts about the demolition of Vishwanath temple and then the construction of a mosque, for example, famous historian Dr. Vishwambhar Nath Pandey in his book 'Bharatiya Sanskriti, Mughal Virasat: Aurangzeb Ke Farman', citing the book 'Feathers and Stones' by Pattabhi Sitaramayya, a renowned scholar and lecturer of Gandhism, writes about Aurangzeb's order and the reason for the demolition of Vishwanath temple, 'Once Aurangzeb was passing through a region near Banaras. All Hindu courtiers along with their families came to Kashi to bathe in the Ganga and visit Vishwanath. When people came out after visiting Vishwanath, they found out that a queen of the king of Kutch was missing. When a search was conducted, the queen was found in the basement below the temple, without clothes and ornaments, frightened. When Aurangzeb came to know about this evil deed of the Pandits, he became very angry and said that where such robbery and rape takes place under the sanctum sanctorum of the temple, it certainly cannot be the house of God. He issued an order to demolish the temple immediately.

"Vishwambhar Nath Pandey writes, 'Aurangzeb's order was immediately followed. But when the queen of Kutch heard about this, she sent a message for Aurangzeb that there is no fault of the temple but it is the pandas of the temple who are at fault.

The queen presented her wish that the temples should be rebuilt. Due to his religious beliefs, it was not possible for Aurangzeb to rebuild the temple and therefore he built a mosque in its place and fulfilled the queen's wish."

"It's really sad," Prof Vachaspati who had returned now, said after listening to Dr Deshmukh. "I feel that the new generation should be taught about this truth because all they have been taught in their textbooks is how brave the Mughals were and how easy it was to plunder the Indians."

"Really professor, a lot of injustice has been done to our culture," Dr Deshmukh said playing with his rings.

"Prof Vachaspati said, you know Roselina, when Aurangzeb's army attacked Kashi Vishwanath temple once again in 1664, the Naga Sadhus, fed up, resisted it for the first time and saved the temple. They defeated Aurangzeb and his army badly. This defeat of the Mughals is mentioned in James G. Lochtefeld's book 'The Illustrated Encyclopaedia of Hinduism', Volume 1. He described this incident in his book as the 'Battle of Gyan Vapi'. It is worth noting that in this description he has called the 'victory' of the Naga Sadhus against Aurangzeb and his army 'Mahan'. Even though this war has been described properly, you cannot imagine how the Naga Sadhus wreaked such havoc on the huge and armed Mughal army that they did not dare to look at Kashi for four years."

Dr Deshmukh was looking at his watch continuously.

"Sir, Kirat has also mention about this in his diary," Rumi said showing the part written in green ink. "He writes that James G. Lochtefeld wrote in his book, 'A battle was reportedly fought in Banaras by Naga ascetic warriors of the great Nirvani Akhara.

According to a handwritten book in the archives of the Akhara, the Akhara's soldiers won a great victory near the Gyan Vapi well in 1664. This document only states that the ascetics were victorious against the forces of the 'Sultan'. However, historians have speculated that this figure was of the Mughal emperor Aurangzeb. If the story is true, then this battle may have been a major factor in Aurangzeb's decision to demolish the Vishwanath temple in 1669. The Naga Sadhus must have retaliated till their last breath. According to local folklore and oral stories, about 40,000 Naga Sadhus sacrificed their lives while protecting the Kashi Vishwanath Jyotirlinga, fighting the Mughal army of lakhs. Islamic robbers have always followed the strategy of deceit and trickery in war and we Hindus did not support those who fought for us, otherwise 40,000 Nagas would have changed the course of India's history, let alone being inscribed in it. If they had received even a little help, they would have sent the Mughal Sultanate to hell there itself.

"When Aurangzeb attacked Varanasi again in 1669, he understood that the temple was linked to the faith and sentiments of Hindus, so he ensured that it was not rebuilt and Gyan Vapi Masjid was built in its place. I must leave now," Dr Deshmukh stood up, looking at his watch. Everyone joined their hands in respect to him.

"It was a pleasure meeting you," said Roselina. Rumi touched his feet and Shekhar and Prof. Vachaspati went to see him off. His car was parked outside the house.

❑

15
Far too many Struggles

It was half past eight. Rumi knew that in an hour her parents would be there to pick her up. "They should also dine with us, you message them," Prof Vachaspati had already told this to Rumi. "Till then Deepshikha would also be here."

It is impossible to say no to him, by now Rumi knew it very well. She could not say no to any request or order of such a kind-hearted person.

Shekhar came into the study and said laughing, "May I also tell something? Although my knowledge is zero in comparison to the two scholar ladies sitting in front of me."

"Don't show off too much," Rumi said patting him on his shoulder.

"You are most welcome Shekhar. Please share," Roselina said very politely.

"If we look at India's history today, we come to know that while our warriors played an important role in fighting the Islamic invaders, the sadhu sanyasis also put their lives on the line for the protection of our temples and religion. If you think about it, the Islamic powers had everything i.e., modern weapon, allurement for conversion, protection of the ruling dispensations. Despite all this, if Hinduism is still thriving today, then apart from the saints of Bhakti Yoga who instilled faith in Ram-Krishna in the common people, the struggle of the sadhus also has a contribution.

"The sanyasis revolted against the East India Company in Bengal as well, which is known as the 'sanyasi rebellion.' It began in 1770 itself, when the British started to collect taxes from the people after the Battle of Buxar. The sanyasis fought armed battles in Murshidabad in Jalpaiguri and the jungles of Baikunthpur. Where on one hand Bankim Chandra Chatterjee has called it the revolution of the Hindus in his book 'Anand Math,' left historians have labelled it as a struggle against imperialism and feudalism. The sanyasis were also included in the army of the Nawab of Bengal and the Rajput kings of Maharashtra. This movement continued for five centuries.

"The description of these Naga Sadhus is also found in the book 'A History of Dashnami Naga Sanyasis' by Jadunath Sarkar, who was a leading historian who wrote about the Mughal dynasty. According to him Naga Sadhus have attained great glory. The war went on from dawn till dusk and the Dashanami Nagas proved themselves to be the heroes. They protected the honour of Vishwanath.

"These are the battles which we know about even though in bits and pieces, but apart from these Naga Sadhus have fought many battles and protected the society and dharma," till then Prof Vachaspati had come back. Deepshikha ji also entered the study with him and everybody's face lit up seeing her. Everyone was inspired by her dignified personality.

"Oh ho! now who is going to listen to me," Prof Vachaspati said laughing.

"I am going from here, we will meet at the dinner table in ten minutes," Deepshikha ji looked at her husband with mischief in her eyes and went out of the room.

"Sir, you trouble ma'am a lot," Shekhar joked.

"All the secrets shall open up to you when you marry Rumi and you will also understand the compulsions of a man," Prof Vachaspati teased him back, "Anyways, we have ten minutes, so, I was telling you about those battles which find nearly no mention. They also fought in Kutch and Bhuj of Gujarat. Monasteries used to be their strongholds and they used to ride on elephants and horses. Spear and trident were their main weapons even then and are so even today. Naga ascetics laid the foundation of Nagaud state in Madhya Pradesh. The rulers there were their worshippers.

"The queen of Jhansi was also supported by Naga Sadhus. Rani Lakshmi Bai's guru was Puranvirathi Peethadheesh Swami Gangadasji Maharaj. When the first organized war against the British began in 1857, Rani Lakshmi Bai came from Datia to Gwalior to ask for help from Scindia, but he did not meet her. While returning from there, her horse could not cross the river Swarn Rekha of Gwalior and fell. At this time, she was shot in her left thigh. Despite this, she killed the enemy soldier by wielding a sword with her left hand. A soldier of the 8th Hussar Army of the English army struck the queen with a sword on her forehead, which cut her head up to the eye. Blood started flowing profusely. But the queen, while falling, showed her bravery once again and cut off the shoulder of that soldier. At this time, the queen's Pathan Sardar Gul Mohammad killed that Hussar soldier.

"The queen's other chieftain Ramchandra Deshmukh and Diwan Raghunath Singh attacked the Hussar soldiers. In such a situation, the Hussar soldiers ran away. After this, the injured queen was taken by her chieftain to the hut of sadhu Ganga Das nearby. Sadhu Ganga Das put holy Ganga water in her mouth. She asked Raghunath Singh where she was. On hearing the name of Ganga Das's Badi Shala, the queen asked him to go to the Shala. When she came to the Guru, she said that 'I will not be able to live now, but do not let my body and my son fall into the hands of the British.' After this, when the British surrounded the Shala from outside, then about two thousand sadhus present in the Shala asked to fight with the queen. Because Naga Sadhus were capable of using weapons and cannons, they helped the queen. In this war, 745 Naga Sadhus were martyred and two sadhus were made to go away from the Shala along with the queen's son. After this, the British destroyed the monastery and looted the property."

"On one hand these brave women and men make us proud, while on the other hand when I think about their sacrifice and giving their blood and life for the protection of nation and religion I shudder. I salute these Indian brave hearts," when Roselina actually did a salute standing up, her eyes were moist.

'What can be a more pleasant feeling than witnessing a girl from a foreign land being proud of Indian history and culture,' Rumi thought and looked at Roselina with appreciative eyes.

"There is another incident of 1857. The bugle against the British had been blown in the whole country. Rumi, I have underlined this part in Kirat's diary, you read it out while I go and help Deepshikha," said Prof. Vachaspati pointing towards Kirat's diary kept on the table and went out.

Rumi picked up the diary and saw that there was a bookmark on one page. It seems that he must have read it while sitting here and put the bookmark. She started reading, "The first flame of the fire of revolution in Mau district of Uttar Pradesh had taken the blood of six British officers in Mau town on 6 June thirteen years before 1857. On 1 April 1858, Thakur Ramat Singh Baghel, the Jagirdar of Mankehari state of Rewa district of Madhya Pradesh, attacked the British camp in Nagaud with about three hundred companions. He killed Major Kellis and captured that place. After this, on 23 May, he headed straight to Naugaon, the then big British camp. But due to the strong strategy of Major Kirk, he could not succeed there. He wanted to go to Jhansi to help Rani Lakshmi Bai, but he had to head towards Chitrakoot. Here Thakur Dalganjan Singh, the Jagirdar of Pindra, along with his army of 1500 soldiers, killed two officers, looted their belongings, and headed towards Chitrakoot on 11 June 1858.

"They had camped on the Hanuman Dhara hill, where Naga Sadhus and saints were helping them. More than three hundred Naga Sadhus were working on the next strategy with the revolutionaries. Then Thakur Ranmat Singh Vaghel, returning from Naugaon, also arrived with his army. At the same time, the kings of Panna and Ajaygarh attacked Hanuman Dhara along with the British army. The then princes also helped the British. Hundreds of sadhus fought with the British along with the revolutionaries. The revolutionaries had to face defeat in this war which lasted for three days. Thakur Dalganjan Singh attained martyrdom here, while Thakur Ranmat Singh was seriously injured. The Hanuman Dhara hill turned red with the blood of the revolutionaries along with about three hundred Sadhus. Why does no one see this sacrifice and sacrifice of the Naga Sadhus?" Rumi became emotional while finishing the part.

"This question is arising in everyone's mind these days," Shekhar said, "but I am sure that when people read your research paper, not only will their doubts about Naga Sadhus be dispelled, but their perspective of looking at them will also change. The fear that arises in people after seeing their naked and terrifying form will also go away."

"When the two of you met Naga Sadhus and that too with many sadhus in the cave for the very first time, were you not scared?" Roselina asked after listening to Shekhar.

"I will not lie to you, it was scary indeed. But as I the conversation with them went further, that fear was replaced by curiosity and then I can go through anything for Rumi," Rumi smiled when Shekhar said this in a dramatic tone.

"I was very scared and Shekhar had lied as well that we were there to become Naga Sadhu and Sadhvi. You mean, I, a Naga Sadhvi, you don't think before speaking Shekhar. Thank God they listened to us patiently and did not chase away from their cave, otherwise their anger is known all across the world." Rumi laughed as she recalled their meeting with the Naga Sadhus.

Hearing this, Shekhar felt embarrassed, as Roselina was looking at him with surprise. To overcome his embarrassment and change the topic, he said, "Naga Sadhus do not get angry without reason. This is the notion of people that needs to be dispelled. People start thinking all sorts of things on seeing them in the Kumbh Mela! They judge them by their external appearance rather than their valour. On hearing the word Naga Sadhu, our sophisticated society thinks of uncivilized and strange saints covered in ashes. However, the British have created this misunderstanding in the name of education and civilization. The main objective of these

British was to keep us away from our glorious history. The truth is that these ascetic warriors or Naga Sadhus fought continuously against foreign invaders including Mughals, Turks, Persians, Afghans, Ghoris and the British. They were committed to maintaining the rich cultural tradition of India."

"You just mentioned Naga Sadhvis, Rumi. I want to know about them too," Roselina, lost in her thoughts, suddenly said, "I was not aware about the existence of Naga Sadhvis."

"I will definitely tell you, but tomorrow. Let Shekhar finish, otherwise he will say that we did not give him a chance to speak. As it is already late." Rumi looked at Shekhar as if to tell him that look, you are also being given a full chance to speak.

Shekhar's mind was turning the pages of history at that time, so straightaway he started off, "During the time of Prithvi Raj Chauhan, when Mohammad Ghori attacked him, the Naga Sadhus surrounded Ghori's army in Kurukshetra even before Prithvi Raj's army reached there. Historians talk about the second battle of Tarain, in which Prithvi Raj Chauhan was defeated, but do not mention the first battle of Tarain which took place in 1191, when Ghori's army was trying to damage the temples of Kurukshetra and Pehowa, how the Naga Sadhus, along with Prithvi Raj's army, cut down Gauri's army in Tarain. After this war, Prithvi Raj Chauhan gave the flag of Hinduism to the Naga Sadhu warrior monks in Kumbh to show respect, because he knew that his rule would end soon and no one could protect this flag better than them. He knew that these Naga Sadhus have always stood in defence of Hinduism.

"Not only this, in the Kumbh Mela that took place after this war, to honour the Naga warriors, Prithvi Raj Chauhan gave them the right to take the first bath in the Kumbh. Since then, it has been a tradition that the Naga Sadhus will take the first bath in the Kumbh Mela," Shekhar said while looking at the books on Prof Vachaspati's bookshelf. Of course, he always had believed on the facts usually based on the science, but the history had upset him at this time. That is why he started flipping through the books to divert his attention. Then suddenly he said, "When the world-famous Maharana Pratap waged a war against the Mughals, the Naga ascetics helped him, after which the Mughals were left stunned. The tombs of the Naga Sadhus who were killed in the war between Chhapali pond and Ranakada Ghat in Panchmahua area of Rajasthan can still be seen today. The proof of the Sadhus' mastery in war is found in a painting of 'Akbarnama', in which two groups of sadhus are fighting with swords.

"The weapons of war and non-violence seem to be opposed to each other. Yet, history is witness to the sage-warriors in Mughal and British India who gave a new dimension to the concept of 'non-violence' by training in the use of war weapons described in ancient Hindu scriptures. And when Taimur Lang came to India…"

"Rumi," when she heard her mother's voice she said, "Let's go out. Mom and Dad have also come. We will talk later. Anyway, it is not right to make Prof Vachaspati and Deepshikha ji wait too long."

❑

16
Naga Sadhvis

'The life of Naga Sadhus is that of courage, freedom and extraordinary discipline.' Kirat had written many such statements in different pages of the diary. Whenever Rumi read through those lines, her heart would fill with more respect for the Naga Sadhus.

"I want to visit all the akharas," when Rumi said this to Shekhar on phone two days later, he was astonished. That time he had his eyes fixed on the screen of his laptop struggling with some software.

"How did this thought come across your mind all of a sudden?"

"What do you mean by thought? It is important that I should mention about the akharas too in detail in my research paper, why are you so surprised? If you don't want to go then I can go alone, or I can also go with Roselina," as if Rumi remembered something and she hung up the phone."

"Very good idea Rumi! I would like to come with you," Roselina said excitedly after hearing Rumi on the phone. "But when?"

"Give me some time, I will check the arrangements. The akharas are situated at different places so which places would be possible for us to cover, we will have to check that."

"Yesterday everybody was busy so we could not meet. I want to know about the incident involving Taimur. Wasn't Shekhar saying something about it the other day?"

"We can meet at the coffee house in Connaught Place. I will bring Kirat's diary with me. Prof Vachaspati has gone to Chandigarh for two days to participate in a seminar."

"Send me the location and I will be there in the evening."

"You look beautiful in saree," Rumi said when she saw Roselina wearing a saree.

"I love Indian dresses," Roselina smiled.

By that time Shekhar had also arrived. Drinking her coffee, Roselina said, "Shekhar, you were telling something about Taimur the other day?"

"I do not know much, just a little bit," Shekhar said. He was somewhat hesitant thinking if he would be able to tell them in correct manner or not.

"Please share," Roselina said eating a piece of pastry.

"Taimur Lung was a ruler in the fourteenth century who founded the Timurid dynasty. It was in year 1398, ruler of Samarkand, Taimur Lung had attacked and plundered Iraq and Iran through central Asia. While returning he reached Afghanistan and there in Kabul a spy came to meet him. That spy had arrived from Delhi. He told the king that the situation in Delhi is not very good. The sultanate in Delhi has gone weak after the death of the king, Feroze Shah Tughlaq in 1388. Many rulers have ascended the throne in this past decade since his death. Assassinations are widespread for the throne. The situation of internal struggle could be taken advantage of and Delhi is is facing the same situation. If successful there will be so much wealth to gain like one he has never seen before.

"Taimur Lung reached Delhi and in fifteen days only his ministers and soldiers ruthlessly plundered Delhi and destroyed the crops. It is said that he left Delhi in such a dire situation that it took hundred years to recover. But whether Delhi was destroyed or ruined was not his concern. He came to Delhi with one purpose - to plunder and he left for Samarkand as soon as he achieved it.

"During his retreat, when he reached Haridwar, after plundering from Meerut and Bijnor to the banks of Ganga, then he started destruction there as well. Timur Lang came to Haridwar during the Haridwar Kumbh Mela of 1398, which fell after 1393 AD. He looted the pilgrims. He destroyed many temples and idols. There was a grand Vishnu temple in Daatwali haweli near Har Ki Pauri. Taimur Lung destroyed it as well. He demolished many temples. At that time, Taimur had an encounter with Naga Sadhus in the battle that was fought in Jwalapur near Haridwar and the Nagas fought with him so hard that he was compelled to flee the battlefield. At the time of Taimur's attack, when most of the kings had gone into hiding out of fear, Mahabali Jograj Singh, the brave son of Dada Mansingh Parmar, the head of Parmar clan and descendant of King Jagdev Parmar, Gurjar and Harveer Jat, captain of the women's army Ram Pyari, Dhuladhadi, etc. along with Naga warriors forced Taimur Lang to flee from India.

"It is said that when he reached the Bhairav temple near Mayadevi temple and hit on the idol of Bhairav Ji, suddenly a swarm of snakes and scorpions appeared out of nowhere. Taimur's army was scared upon seeing so many snakes and scorpions and there was a stampede in the army. Even Taimur himself was scared to death when he saw this army of snakes and scorpions.

"Hearing all this makes my heart sad," Roselina said, "How angry you must feel, India is your country and all this must sting a lot to you."

"We cannot change the history, but we can always try to save our present and future," Rumi said looking at Shekhar.

"You are right, shall we go now?"

Both stood up when Shekhar asked.

"Roselina, if you wish you can stay at my home tonight. We can discuss a lot of things and can also make plans to go and visit the akharas."

"Sure," Roselina's face lit up at Rumi's proposal. "I too will get a chance to read your notes and Kirat's diary."

"So, its decided then, I will drop you both at her home. I have brought my car today. My brother had kept it in his possession for so many days."

"Before that we will have to go to the hotel, I will pick few of my clothes."

Roselina has already met Rumi's parents at Prof. Vachaspati's house. After talking and making plans with them, both went and sat in Rumi's room. Arrangements had been made for Roselina to sleep in the guest room. Seeing her wearing a loose orange nightie, Rumi joked, "Do you also want to become a Naga Sadhvi? You are wearing the same saffron coloured clothes, girl!"

"No, no. Like you I also have a boyfriend, so there is no chance of becoming a Sadhvi."

They kept laughing for a long time at this joke.

"This reminded me. Rumi, you wanted to tell me something about Naga Sadhvis the other day. Has Kirat also written anything about them? Or have you ever met them?"

"Kirat has written about them, but very little. I have never met Naga Sadhvis, but I have seen their videos on YouTube and have written something based on that. But I will meet them for sure when I go to the Kumbh Mela."

"Maybe they would not have to follow strict rules like Naga Sadhus or the process to become a Sadhvi may not be as complicated and tough as one has to go through to become a Naga Sadhu?"

"It is not like that at all, Roselina. A woman has to follow the same strict procedures as a man to become a Naga Sadhvi. Every procedure that men follow, women also have to follow. The only difference is that female Nagas can wear orange or red coloured clothes on their body. They wear a tilak on their forehead. They have to do hard penance for years, have to do their own pind-daan while alive, have to shave their head and only then they become female Naga Sadhus. Naga Sadhvis chant the name of God upon waking up and before going to sleep. During the Kumbh Mela, Naga Sadhvis also wear clothes and take a dip in the holy water.

"These Naga Sadhvis live in the jungles, caves and hills, away from the world and they are always engrossed in the devotion of God. After the completion of tough tests, a female Naga is given the stature of Maa. Apart from this, they are also called by some other names like Nagin, Avadhootani etc. There are female Naga Sadhus in Mai Bada, which has now been named Dashnam Sanyasini Akhara after giving it a detailed form. They are also given the title of 'Srimahant' as the head of a particular area. Women elected to the post of Shrimahant travel in a palanquin during the royal bath. Also, they are allowed to put the flag of the Akhara, drum and dana below their religious flag."

"Amazing," Roselina's eyes widened with surprise. "Do these sadhvis also keep dreadlocks and wrap ashes on their bodies? They wear clothes, so they must not apply ashes, right?"

"Female Nagas do not keep dreadlocks, but they have to pluck their hair with their own hands. They apply a tilak on their forehead and smear ashes on their bodies, and just wear a saffron-coloured cloth. Their cloth is unstitched. This cloth is called 'Ganti'. They too appear in front of the world only on special occasions like Kumbh-Maha Kumbh. After bathing in the holy rivers, they soon disappear. This is the reason why very few people get to see female Naga Sadhus. Even there are very few photos of female Naga Sadhus on the Internet.

"Before becoming a Naga Sadhvis, the woman's house, family and even the every aspect, minute details of her previous life is also examined. Before becoming a Naga Sadhvis or Sanyasin, the female sadhu has to prove that she no longer has any relationship with her family and society. Only after this, the Acharya gives initiation to the woman. After this, she takes off her worldly clothes and wears yellow clothes. The female sadhu also removes her hair and performs her own pind-daan. After this, the Naga Sadhvis start their sadhana after taking a bath in the river and purifying themselves. The Naga Sadhvis chants the name of

God the whole day and wakes up in the Brahma Muhurta in the morning and chants the name of Lord Shiva. In the evening, they worship Lord Dattatreya. After lunch, they chant the name of Lord Shiva."

"So, are many things asked of those who wish to become Naga Sadhu or Sadhvi? I mean, is there a proper interview?" Rumi laughed after hearing Roselina's question.

"You can say that. Many kinds of questions are asked of them. I will tell you some. I had read about them in a book. Wait, maybe I have their recordings too." Rumi started looking at her phone. She played an audio.

Who is your sister, cousin, who is your mother?
Who will walk beside you, will anyone bother?

Fire (dhuni) is my cousin, fire is my sister
This earth is my mother
Vibhuti will accompany us
The night will talk to us

Where is your home, where do you come from?
Who are your mother and father what did they give you name?

Sky is our home
In the nether world we remain
We are the child of Alakh Purush
Truth is our name

I shall give up the seat, bind this beautiful body with bracelet
I shall tie you, I shall tie you guru, where did you get this yoga from
I Give up the seat, I give up the bracelet

I Give up this beautiful body
I Give up my self
I Give up my guru
Agam gave me this Yoga

Who gave you this pot, who gave you this bag?
Who gave you this saffron attire, who is the man / woman celibate?

Brahma gave me this pot
Vishnu gave me this bag
Mahadev gave the saffron dress
Alakh, all the man and women celibate

You are a Naga, I am a Naga, let's go to the Kumbh Mela
Tell me the tree without bark and I shall be your disciple

I am a naga, you are a naga,
lets go to the Kumbh mela
Hairs are the trees without bark
And now I am the guru and you are the disciple

Rumi could not tell how much could Roselina understand, but the puzzled look on her face told her that she was amazed.

Listening to Roselina, Rumi opened Kirat's diary and began reading, "In 2013, despite strong opposition from Akharas and Shankaracharyas, the fourteenth and first women's Akhara of the country was formed. Female Shankaracharya Trikal Bhavanta established a women's Akhara named 'Shri Sarveshwar Mahadev Baikunth Dham Mukti Dwar Akhara'. According to the manifesto of the Akhara, Adi Shakti Vedmata Gayatri was declared the goddess of the Akhara and Lord Dattatreya was declared the

Acharya of the Akhara. Then the leader of the Naga Mahila Akhara was Divya Giri, who had completed her studies of medical technician from the Institute of Public Health and Hygiene, New Delhi before becoming a Sadhu. In the year 2004, she officially became a female Naga Sadhu. Then she said that we want to do things differently.

"'The most adored deity of the Juna Akhara is Lord Dattatreya, we want to make Anusuya, the mother of Dattatreya, our most adored deity. Anusuya is the name of the mother of sage Atri and Lord Dattatreya. She was famous all over the world for her devotion to her husband. While the wives of Brahma, Mahesh and Vishnu felt that they were the most faithful to their husbands, when Maharishi Narad told all three that Anusuya was more faithful to her husband on earth than them, all three were deeply hurt. All three told their husbands that Anusuya should be tested. Finally, Brahma, Vishnu and Mahesh had to go to test her. This test was such that the status of Mata Anusuya as a goddess became very high. All three disguised themselves as sages and reached Anusuya. When Mata Anasuya started serving food, all three gods said that they were saints, you will have to accept whatever we say. The sages said that you will have to serve food naked. On hearing this, she said that if I have fulfilled my duty as a faithful wife then turn these three gods into children. All three of them became six-month old babies. Anusuya fed milk to all three and also fulfilled her duty as a faithful wife. This is the reason why for most Naga women sages, after Shiva and Dattatreya, Mata Anusuya is not only their idol but they also worship her as a goddess.

"When I asked the head of the Mahila Akhara, Trikal Bhavanta, why the need for a Mahila Akhara was felt, she said, "The need to form this Akhara arose due to many reasons. The 13

Akharas formed so far may have been giving respect and place to women, but like other institutions of the society, women are exploited in these as well, they do not get the place they should get. Adi Shankaracharya had formed only four Akharas, but due to mutual differences and differences in opinions, 13 Akharas have been formed in the country today. She said that when 4 to 13 Akharas can be formed, then what is the problem in forming the fourteenth one."

"The more I am learning about these Naga Sadhus and Sadhvis, the more I feel as if I am entering into some mysterious world. Now I understand why even foreigners are getting attracted to the Naga Sadhu - Sadhvi tradition. There are many European women among the female Nagas," Roselina said yawning. "We should go to sleep."

"Good night," said Roselina and went to the guest room to sleep.

❑

17
Meeting with the Mahant

Next morning before leaving for Haridwar with Rumi, Roselina went to the hotel, packed the essentials in a bag and picked up her camera, tripod and laptop.

"We will back by tonight, right?" Roselina asked.

Rumi smiled and put her hands on hers to reassure her. She had asked this question more than once since they had made the plan to go to Haridwar yesterday.

"Don't worry. You can finish your other works tomorrow."

"It is so sudden you know. Otherwise, I had planned to stay in India for one more week. But Mom wants me to come back immediately. I am worried for her. There must be some reason, otherwise she would have never called me," there was panic in Roselina's voice.

"Roselina, everything will be alright. Be positive." Rumi too was upset about Roselina's abrupt return.

Suddenly the phone rang. "What happened? Why so sudden plan to go to Haridwar? I know I had said what was the need to go to visit the akharas but do you really think I would have let you go alone? It was possible for me to go with you only on the weekends, couldn't you wait for 2 more days?"

"Oh now don't be angry. Actually Roselina has to leave for California day after tomorrow. So she asked if she could visit at least one akhara before she leaves. That is why we are going to Haridwar. The main Juna Akhara is there only. I hope we get to meet the Mahamandaleshwar or some Mahant there. I have also sent a message to Prof Vachaspati."

"Ok take care." Shekhar said and hung up the phone.

Rumi started reading Kirat's diary in the cab. Roselina was listening to her very attentively. 'I got to know many interesting things when I visited the akharas. At that time I did not know that the attire, activities, ways of devotion etc of a Naga Sadhu is determined according to the akhara he is associated with. Primarily there are 13 akharas who have been granted recognition out of which 7 are Shaiva, 3 Vaishnava and 3 are Udasin. Although a Kinnar akhara has also been established. From the outside these akharas look the same but their traditions and methods are quite different.'

"What does Kinnar mean?" Roslina asked.

"Third gender," Rumi said and began reading, 'The names of these akharas are - Shri Juna Akhara, Shri Atal Akhara, Shri Aahwan Akhara, Shri Niranjani Akhara, Shri Panchagni Akhara, Shri Nagpanthi Gorakhnath Akhara, Shri Vaishnav Akhara, Shri Mahanirvani Akhara, Shri Nirmohi Akhara, Shri Panchayati Bada Udasin Akhara, Shri Panchayati Naya Udasin Akhara, Shri Nirmal Akhara and Shri Panch Digambar Ani Akhara.

'Juna means old. It is the oldest Akhara. Currently, the highest number of Mahamandaleshwars belong to this Akhara, which includes foreigners and female Mahamandaleshwars as well. It is also called Bhairav Akhara. Rudravatar Dattatreya is their Ishta dev. When I went to his ashram near Haridwar's Maya Mandir, I found out that Juna Akhara was established in 1145 in Karna Prayag in Uttarakhand state. This Akhara is also known as Bhairav Akhara. Its centre is believed to be at Hanuman Ghat in Varanasi. There are more than five lakh Naga Sadhus and Mahamandleshwar Sanyasi in this Akhara. In this Akhara, there are Mahants according to different regions, who look after the work according to their respective regions.'

After reaching Haridwar, they first stopped the cab at a dhaba and ate hot tandoori roti and daal. Roselina was relishing it. She liked the chilli and carrot pickle very much. Although eating chilli brought tears in her eyes, but she was eating with great pleasure.

When they reached the ashram of Juna Akhara, it was already afternoon. After a lot of requests, they got the opportunity to meet Mahant Shiv Giri of Juna Akhara. Rumi and Roselina sat down on the ground in front of him.

"You can sit on the chair if you want." Rumi shook her head to refuse and sat on the carpet spread on the floor.

"You said that you are doing research on Naga Sadhus, it all right but why?" There was a harshness in Mahant Shiv Giri's voice. "Civic society's opinion of us is not very good, so why are you so curious to know about us? It has become a trend these days. Many authors and journalists come here to meet us."

"My research paper will be an attempt to change the opinion formed in the society about you people," Rumi said very politely. "And Roselina also wants to take a positive message to her country."

After remaining silent for some time, he said, "Ask what you want to know?" This time his voice was flat but expressive and neutral like he is.

"Does the Juna Akhara have any system? I mean Akharas?" Roselina had turned on her recorder.

"Akhara is associated with a distinct system. After India gained independence, these akharas gave up their military character. The heads of these akharas insisted that their followers lead a disciplined life by studying and following the Sanatani values of Indian culture and philosophy. In fact, akharas are a kind of boarding, lodging, and training place for sadhus and sanyasis. Here sadhus stay, food and drink are arranged and they get training in different activities of sanyasi. In these akharas, the tradition of Guru-Shishya is taken care of completely. The disciple sadhu or sanyasi gives the status of God to his Guru and his instructions are no less than a 'royal order.'

"The Mahant is placed as the chief of each of the 13 major akharas. Look at it like this, that this Shri Panch Dashnam Juna Akhara is a whole society, where a committee of all the heads of 52 families of sadhus is formed. All of them elect the Sabhapati for the Akhara. Once elected, the post of Sabhapati remains with him for life. Who will be the Sabhapati, it is decided only during the Kumbh Mela. The Akhara has four Madhis (small temples), in which the Mahant, Kasht Kaushal Mahant and Kotwal are appointed. The current Mahamandleshwar Acharya Avdheshanand Ji Maharaj was elected during the Kumbh of 1998. He holds this post for life. Apart from being a spiritual guru, he is also a great saint and writer of Hindu religion. Swamiji has given initiation to more than 10 lakh sanyasis in the Akhara."

"Ten lakhs? Oh my God!" Roselina said suddenly.

Shiv Giri Mahant continued unperturbed, “In this Akhara, members of Ramta Panch are also appointed. Their work is to worship their Ishta Devta and protect the Akhara. They are also called fellow (chal sadasya) members. Out of thirteen Akharas, only seven Sanyasi Akharas make Naga Sadhus, that is, Juna, Mahanirvani, Niranjani, Atal, Ani, Anand and out of thirteen Akharas, only seven Sanyasi Akharas make Naga Sadhus – these are Juna, Mahanirvani, Niranjani, Atal, Ani, Anand and Aahwan Akhara.

“Juna akhara does a lot of work for social reforms as well. When the Supreme Court of India granted recognition to the Kinnar akhara in the form of third gender, with a purpose to bring them into mainstream, this akhara not only gave them a place in their akhara but also gave them an opportunity to raise their own flag of dharma and also take the royal bath.

“With their war skills, the sages of Juna akhara compelled the Nizam of Junagarh in Rajasthan to surrender in the battle. The Mughal army had to flee the battlefield when they encountered the valour of the sanyasis. After this the Nizam called the sanyasis for a truce and deceitfully poisoned their food, but as it was the custom, the priest, Kothari and the sanyasis deployed on watch duty did not eat that food. They were saved and it was them who later established the Panch Dashnama Juna Akhara.

“You both must be aware that to become a sanyasi in the akhara one has to fulfil the pledge of 12 years. The one who takes the pledge, is called a Brahmachari for 12 years. During that time, he is taught about the customs and rules of the akhara. When the brahmachari fulfils the pledge for 12 years, then he is initiated as a Naga Sadhu during the Kumbh Mela. Naga Sanyasis observe restraint in what they eat and what they think. Naga sanyasis display their status by wearing trident, sword, conch and Rudraksha etc.

"Most of the ashrams of Juna Akhara are in remote areas. It is very difficult to live there, but the sanyasis of the Akhara live in these places amid strict discipline. Female Naga Sadhvis get full respect in the Akhara as well."

"I want to ask you some questions?" Roselina said.

"I think I have already answered everything."

"Actually, if you don't have any problem, I want to make a video. You may feel that I am asking a question again, but they will be necessary for the video," Roselina asked hesitantly.

"Okay."

Roselina started setting up the camera to make the video.

"How many Mahamandaleshwars are there in Juna Akhara?"

"There are 800 Mahamandaleshwars of Juna Akhara across the country. Currently, the highest post of the Akhara is held by Acharya Mahamandaleshwar Swami Avdheshanand Giri Maharaj."

"What do you mean by Mahamandaleshwar?"

"Mahamadaleshwar is a title popular among the ancient kings which is dedicated to a great king. A king who is invincible is known as Mahamadaleshwar. At present this is a title which is given by the sages to the sages, which alleviates them to a higher order among the priests. Such a title is called Mahamandaleshwar."

"How many types of Akharas are there?"

"There are 13 types of Akharas. Sadhus of different traditions are associated with these 13 Akharas, out of which seven Akharas belong to the Shaiv sect. Three Akharas belong to the Vaishnava sect and three Akharas belong to the Udasi sect. These Akharas play a major role in the organization of Kumbh and Ardh Kumbh. Currently, there are only Akharas of the Shaiv, Vaishnava and Udasi sects."

"How are Mahamandaleshwars made?"

"It is very important to have many qualifications to become Mahamandaleshwar. First, one should have the knowledge of Sanskrit and Vedas - Puranas, should be a Sanyasi, should not have a family or family ties. There is no age limit, but it is very important to have knowledge of Vedas. It is important for a person to have renunciation."

"What positions I mean what are ranks of Naga Sadhus?"

"I will tell you the positions in sequence from top to bottom. The biggest position is of Acharya Mahamandaleshwar, then Mahamandaleshwar, Digambarshree, Peer Mahant, Thanapati Mahant, Jampatia Mahant, Shri Mahant and Mahant, i.e., like I am a Mahant."

"Tell me something about Kinnar Akhara."

"I am glad you asked this question. It is newly founded akhara which did not have the right to take the royal bath. But in year 2019, for the first time, on the call of Mahamandaleshwar Shri Laxmi Narayan Tripathi of Kinnar Akhara, this Akhara took a royal bath along with Juna Akhara, at the Kumbh Mela in Haridwar. The Kinnar community, standing at the crossroads of existence, away from culture and society, was crowned in the Mela of religion itself. It was an amazing scene. As soon as the Kinnar Sanyasis entered the Sangam with the sound of conch, it was as if the centuries-old pages written on culture were turned. All the four directions, nature and hymns witnessed these moments of affection in the lap of the Ganga. It was as if religion extended its arms like a mother and embraced these people, neglected for ages.

"The new chapter in the culture that was written after the bath of the Kinnar Akhara shall remain etched in minds forever. Kinnars have participated in devi temples in activities like the shringar of Devi and Badhai Geet. However, years ago Tulsidas Ji had clarified their role through 'Dev Danuj Kinnar Nar Shreni, Sadar Majjhi Sakal Triveni'. Still, their rights embroiled in discussion were confirmed in the Mela of culture and spirituality. The sequence of arrival of Akharas started from six in the morning. The procession of saints and sanyasis along with Naga Sadhus landed on the banks one by one and took bath in the Ganga with chanting of mantras. After this, Mai Bada along with Juna Akhara, then Kinnar Akhara with its mark and identity moved towards the Sangam. As they were moving forward, the steps of every devotee passing by were stopping to see them. Amidst the sun and shivers, faith emerged victorious after a battle of five hours to capture that historic moment in the memory. A large crowd of devotees reached the bank with Bhavani and Guru Mata along with Mahamandaleshwar Laxmi Narayan Tripathi of Kinnar Akhara, dressed in a red sari. As soon as they entered the Ganga, the years - long struggle for the mainstream took a dip with the sound of Bam - Bam Bhole... Jai - Jai Shiv... and thus, amidst the waves of religion, a neglected society was anointed with tilak. The Ganga also began to float a little higher and through their footsteps, this moment was captured in the history of Kumbh."

Rumi and Roselina just kept gazing at Mahant Shiv Giri.

"It is time for my meditation." He said and left.

Rumi came outside and asked, "Can we meet some else at this time?"

"Roam around and see for yourself if anybody is free," a sadhu who was sitting there said.

It was evening. They looked around. No one was found. The Maya temple was open. They could not understand whom to ask.

"I think we should leave." Roselina said.

"Let us go to the temple. Maybe we find someone there who can give us some more information." Rumi had a ray of hope. "You know Roselina, it is believed that the heart and navel of Goddess Sati, i.e. Parvati, the wife of Lord Shiva, fell in the area where the temple is today and hence it is called a Shakti Peeth. Goddess Maya is the presiding deity of Haridwar. She is a three-headed and four-armed goddess, believed to be an incarnation of Shakti. The temple is a Siddha Peetha, a place of worship where wishes are fulfilled. It is one of three such Peethas located in Haridwar, the other two being Chandi Devi Temple and Mansa Devi Temple. According to Hindu mythology, Sati immolated herself to avenge her father's abusive behaviour towards her husband. When Lord Shiva found out that Sati killed herself to preserve his honour, he became furious. An angry Shiva travelled all over the universe carrying Sati's dead body. During this journey, various parts of Sati's body fell at different places. Hindus believe that Sati's navel and heart were found at the same place where the Maya Devi temple in Haridwar stands today."

There was no crowd in the temple at that time. There was a priest who was offering prasad and charnamrit to the visitors.

"Can you tell us something about the Naga Sadhus or the akharas?" Rumi asked, to which he replied curtly, "What could I tell you? In front of you is the ashram of Juna Akhara, go there. But you won't find anybody in the ashram at this hour."

The Naga Story

While returning, Roselina dozed off in the cab, so Rumi started reading Kirat's diary. It had brief descriptions of other Akharas written in it. She started reading, 'Atal Akhara was established in 569 AD in the Gondwana region. Lord Ganesha is their presiding deity. Its main seat is in Patan. Only Brahmins, Kshatriyas and Vaishyas get initiation in this Akhara, other castes are not taken into this Akhara. Aahwan Akhara is believed to have been established in 646 AD, which was reorganized in 1603. The centre of this Akhara is in Kashi. Its presiding deities are both Shri Dattatreya and Shri Gajanan. The main ashram of this Akhara has been established in Rishikesh. This Akhara prohibits the initiation of sadhvis.

'Niranjani Akhara has 50 Mahamandaleshwars. Niranjani Akhara is the most educated Akhara among the 14 Akharas. Established in 826 AD in Mandvi, Gujarat, Niranjani Akhara has Lord Shankar's son Kartikeya as its presiding deity. Niranjani Akhara has Digambar, Sadhu, Mahant and Mahamandaleshwar positions. In India, it has branches in Allahabad, Ujjain, Haridwar, Trimbakeshwar and Udaipur. Panchagni Akhara was established in 1136. Gayatri is its presiding deity. Kashi is its main centre. Shankaracharya of all the four Peethas are among its members. Only Brahmins are given initiation in this Akhara. Besides being a Brahmin, it is also necessary for them to be celibate.

'The Gorakhnath Akhara of the Naga tradition, famous for being naked and adept in the art of war and the tradition of Hatha Yoga, consists of 12 sects. The Gorakhnath Akhara, established at the Ahilya Godavari Sangam, was founded in 866. This Akhara is famous by the name of Yogini Kaul sect. The Vaishnav Akhara was established in 1595 in Daraganj by Shri Madhya Murari. Till the year 1839, the royal bath of this Akhara used to take place in Trimbakeshwar, but after 1848, due to a dispute among the Vaishnav Sadhus, they took bath at Chakratirtha near Trimbakeshear.'

Roselina opened her eyes and seeing Rumi reading the diary, she said, "Please read it out to me too. You know I cannot read Hindi properly."

Rumi smiled and started reading, "Mahanirvani Akhara was established in 671 AD. Some people believe that he was born in Baijnath Dham of Bihar- Jharkhand, while some believe that his birthplace was near Neel Dhara in Haridwar. His favourite deity is Kapil Mahamuni. Mahanirvani Akhara worships Mahakaleshwar Jyotirlinga which has been in existence since ancient times.

"The sadhus of Nirmohi Akhara which was established by Shri Ramanandacharya in 1720, are very mysterious. The monastery and temple of this Akhara are in Uttar Pradesh, Uttarakhand, Madhya Pradesh, Rajasthan, Gujarat and Bihar. In olden times, its followers were also taught archery and swordsmanship. The founder of Bada Udasin Akhara is Shri Chandracharya Udasin. The purpose of this Akhara is to serve. There are 4 Mahants in this Akhara, who never retire.

"Shri Panchayati Naya Udasin Akhara was established by some sadhus of Shri Panchayati Bada Udasin Akhara. In this Akhara, only those who are between 8 to 12 years of age, precisely those who have not grown a beard or moustache are made Nagas. The main centre of Anand Akhara, established in 855 in Berar, Madhya Pradesh, is believed to be in Varanasi. The royal bath of this Akhara takes place along with Aahwan Akhara. Along with dressing up attractively and performing the tandava of Lord Shiva, the sadhus of this Akhara are considered to be the symbol of wealth, power and prosperity.

"Shri Panch Digambar Ani Akhara has the highest number of Khalsa. In the Akharas of the Vaishnav sect, it is called King."

Rumi started feeling sleepy, so she gave the diary to Roselina and rested her head on the seat and closed her eyes. She was thinking how mysterious and enigmatic the world of these Naga Sadhus really is. It is a tough life, but they live it happily, because they have accepted it happily without any compulsion.

❑

18
Ash from the Crematorium

Roselina had gone back to California. As Rumi had spent a wonderful time with her, so she had started to feel the void. They had developed a bond greater than friendship. When Roselina was leaving, both cried and hugged each other as if they had known each other for many years. Prof Vachaspati had returned, but could not get the time to meet Roselina. The research paper was almost complete but still Rumi always strived to find some new aspect. Prof Vachaspati had given her some parts of a book to her. He had found that book in library, but the sad thing was that some pages related to Akharas were torn out.

"Despite giving so many instructions some students do not give up tearing pages from books. Instead of labouring hard, they want to take the shortcut," he said in anger.

Whatever part remained, Rumi began to read, 'The akharas have magnificently played the role of not the saviours but also the promoters of dharma. Akharas of all sects - Shaiva, Vaishnava, Udasi and Nirmal - made a significant contribution in propagating the religion and philosophy of their respective sects. By the end of the eighteenth century, the roots of British rule had started to take hold in the country and in the latter half of the nineteenth century, they took complete control of India. Due to the tough resistance of the British, the political and economic role of Shaiva and Vaishnava Naga Sadhus gradually ended and they got completely involved in the work of religious propagation and social service. After the tradition of Mandaleshwars started in the Dashnami Akharas in the beginning of the nineteenth century, the work of religious propagation intensified. To protect Hinduism from the attacks by Christian missionaries and independent Indian thinkers, it was considered necessary to produce such learned interpreters of Hinduism who could answer their attacks. Hindus could not remain neutral for long and watch the attacks of other sects as silent spectators, it was necessary to protect Hinduism properly through knowledge and philosophy. It became necessary for the armed and weapon-bearing monks to play the role of teachers and preachers for the success of this new work while living in their monasteries and touring.'

'Therefore, it was decided that centres of Sanskrit learning and religious education should be established under the supervision of the most eminent scholars of this sect and groups of able sannyasis should be prepared to propagate religion among the people. This was the right way to respond to the disputes of other sects. Swami Sadanand Giri presents another account of the rise of Mandaleshwars according to which Mandaleshwars originated in the middle of the nineteenth century as per the suggestion of respected Swami Dhanraj Giri of Kailash Ashram Rishikesh as Acharya Gurus, whose work was to explain the path and means for initiation into Sannyas. At present, it is a matter of controversy as to what was the main reason for the origin of Mandaleshwars, but there is no doubt that these Mandaleshwars, who are called Mahamandaleshwars in modern times, have been very learned and have been selected from the most able sannyasis of the Dashnami sect.'

Even this much information was enough for her.

In the evening, she was watching TV and suddenly she saw a character playing the role of a Naga Sadhu in the serial, whose makeup left her stunned. She had heard that Naga Sadhus also like to beautify themselves. The only difference is that the makeup items of Nagas are completely different from the cosmetics of women. They are as concerned about their looks and style as the common man. They beat even women with their makeup.

Rumi opened the laptop and started searching on Google. At one place it was mentioned what a Naga Sadhu Premanand Giri had said that 'Nagas have their own special makeup items. These are different from the common world, but Nagas love to dress up.'

"What are you searching for?" Manohar Dave asked as he came into her room.

"Papa, I watched just now on the TV that Naga Sadhus adorn themselves up in many ways. They do so only during the Kumbh Mela. Although not all sadhus like to do so. I am researching that."

"How curious! Tell me more about it."

"Really papa, you will listen to it."

"Why only papa, even I would like to know more about this," Maa said handing them their cups of coffee and sat on a chair beside Rumi.

Rumi began to read, "Every Naga Sadhu has his own style and gloss. Many are quite fierce in their conduct, but 17 types of shringar is the integral part of every Naga Sadhu. It is something that is followed religiously before going for the royal bath. Nagas first adorn themselves, then they pray to their respective deities and gurus and then they go for the royal bath. On top of the 17 shringaras they put on a loincloth, ash, sandalwood, iron or silver bangles also called kara, garland of flowers and Rudraksha beads which are considered an auspicious unit. They also carry a damru, tongs and a vessel or kamandal as other ornaments."

"Nagas claim that other people take a dip in Ganga to purify themselves but this is how they purify themselves before taking the dip in Ganga. Scholars believe that Nagas have a pure heart and are very simple by nature. They are playful in their akhara and it is like their den where they make the atmosphere lively.

"Before adornment and the royal bath, Naga Sadhus stay awake for the entire night and pray to God Shiva. They also pray to the deity of their akhara. According to them, each element of the adornment has a physiological, astrological and yogic interpretation.

"The tilak represents the official deity of the specific akhara. If for the Awahan akhara it is a symbol of Ganesha, for the Juna it symbolises Maharaja Dattatreya. The tilak and its position are also symbolic. It is claimed that its placement in the middle of the forehead, between the eyebrows, is relevant, as it is the point of the Agya chakra of the body. It is believed that applying a tilak increases concentration. Tikka, Damru, Trishul, Tilak, rooted hair, all these are symbols showing that a person is a follower of Shiva.

"This tradition of adornment began when this community used to be a fighting force. Nagas were warriors, who were raised to protect the Sanatan Dharma. Like any other army they have their unique style of getting ready and display their prowess. Dandeshwar Vidhanam are the rules prepared by Adi Shankaracharya which prescribes the adornment that is worn by a Naga Sadhu.

"Interestingly, the seventeenth item in the list of adornments of Naga Sadhus is the Bhasma or ash, which they claim sets them apart from the rest of the world. It gives them a unique identity. They believe that Bhasma or Bhabhut establishes their union with the supreme deity. Adornment or Shringar is a ritual for them that not only displays pride and strength, but also keeps alive a centuries-old tradition.

"They get the ashes from the crematorium or they prepare it themselves. But this bhabhut is prepared after a very long process. Peepal, Pakkad, Rasala, Belpatra, Banana and cow dung are burnt in the Havan Kund. The ash of this burnt material is filtered through a cloth and balls of ash are prepared with raw milk. It is heated in fire seven times and then extinguished with raw milk. This ash is the apparel of Naga Sadhus. This ash also protects them from many calamities."

"It is indeed difficult for a common man to understand how some of the simplest people also have so many complexities hidden in them. I think Naga Sadhus have both simple and complex shades. There are many mysteries surrounding them and no matter how much we try to know them, those mysteries will always be there," her father said.

"Now, tell me in detail about their makeup items, beta," seeing mother's curiosity, both Rumi and Papa started laughing.

"Your mother has also started taking interest in your research. Now at least you will not be scolded that what are you doing, get married soon."

"Do you know anything else except making fun of me? Okay, I will go out."

"Ma, please don't go. I will tell you in detail."

Rumi started to search again and said, "Bhasma is the most favourite thing for Naga Sadhus. Everybody is familiar with God Shiva wearing bhasma on his body in his aughad form. Similarly, the sadhus from Shaiva sect also smear ash, which is very liked by their deity on their body. Every day after the bath Naga Sadhus smear fresh ash on their body."

"Bhasma acts as clothes on their body. But those who make fun of them after seeing them in this form do not think about how they must be enduring cold, heat, rain or any other situation on their body. After all, they are able to do this only because of the strength of their penance and yogic practices. So, they are not ordinary people or Sadhus, right?" Hearing the profound thing that mother had said, Rumi said, "Ma, you are right, but it is not easy to change the viewpoint of the common people. Still, I will keep trying. Everyone should know about the contribution of these Naga Sadhus."

"What are the adornments?" her father asked.

Rumi said, "Many Naga Sadhus wear flower garlands regularly. They like marigold the most. Reason being that marigold flowers remain fresh for a long time. Naga Sadhus wear flowers in their neck, wrists and especially in their matted locks. Since the tilak is both identity and a symbol of power for them, therefore they give most attention to their tilak. Naga Sadhus are very cautious about their tilak, it has to look the same every day. They never change the style of their tilak. The amount of effort and finesse they put in applying tilak could put even the best make-up artist to shame. The reason behind applying the tilak is that there is an Agya Chakra in the middle of our brain, which is also called Guru Chakra. It is called Guru Chakra because it is the place of Brihaspati, the Guru of the Gods. Guru helps in bringing concentration and awakening knowledge. Sadhus who are also ascetics and want to attain divine knowledge by doing hard sadhana, apply tilak at that place to keep the Guru Chakra awakened. For them, this is also a way of expressing respect towards their Guru.

"Just like the Bhasma, the Rudraksh is also very dear to them. It is believed that Rudraksh originated from the tears of Lord Shiva. It is a symbol of Lord Shiva himself. This is why all the Shaiva sadhus wear garland made of Rudraksh beads.

These are not some ordinary beads. They are perfected over many years and it is done so by their meditation and penance. After that it gets some powers and these beads create an atmosphere which becomes the aura of the Sadhu. Rudraksh also works as in acupressure. It exerts pressure on the veins of neck which helps in regulating the blood pressure. With the help of these Rudraksh sadhu adapt themselves to any temperature. This is why when sometimes a sadhu is pleased with a devotee he gives them his Rudraksh as his blessings.

"It is said that if a Naga Sadhu gets pleased and gives his Rudraksh beads to someone, that person considers himself lucky.

"Normally Naga Sadhus remain naked, but many Naga Sadhus wear loincloth as well. Their main objective is that the devotees should not be scared while coming to them. Many sadhus take up different loincloths such as iron loincloths, silver loincloths, wooden loincloths as part of their Hatha yoga. This is also like a penance. Naga Sadhus carry a sword, axe or trident with them. These weapons are not only proof of them being warriors, but are also a part of their adornment. It is also essential for them to have tongs. Tongs are used the most in lighting fire. Tongs are both a weapon and a tool. It is an important part of their personality. Many Naga Sadhus also wear garlands of gems, but such Nagas are rare, because they are not attracted to wealth, but these gems are an essential part of their adornment."

"Wow! It looks like some interesting session is going on. But without me?" It was Shekhar.

"Look whom I brought with me?" All three of them turned their heads. A tall man was standing beside Shekhar. He sported beard and thin moustache. He was wearing a kurta pyjama and a camera was hanging from his neck.

"Let us go and sit in the drawing room." Manohar Dave said while standing from his seat. All of them would not accommodate in that room.

Sitting on the sofa with that man Shekhar said, "He is Shridhar. He works in our Chennai branch. He is an engineer but pursues photography as his hobby and he is a traveller too. A few days ago, when he went to Trimbakeshwar, he got to meet Naga Sadhus. He had also made a documentary on them. Shridhar would be able to tell us a lot more."

"Hello Shridhar, it is nice to meet you," Rumi said

"You should dine with us tonight," Maa said immediately.

"Thank you! I love north Indian food." Shridhar accent had a southern touch in but his pronunciation were very clear. "Please continue what you were doing."

"You have come to our house for the first time. Why do you want to get bored with me? I will tell mom and dad later. Let's talk about something else now."

"No, I will not get bored at all. Shekhar told you that I have made a documentary on Naga Sadhus. Whatever you tell me will definitely increase my knowledge."

Rumi began speaking, "Their matted hair is one of the marks of identification for Naga Sadhus. They either wrap their tangled long hair and tie it or keep it open. There are many reasons behind this, but the most logical reason is that dreadlocks are the recognition of the intention to separate from the physical body. Naga Sadhus want to attain salvation and that is why they do penance and meditation. In such a situation, they do not spend much time in such things which may take up their time of meditation. They do not like to groom or comb their hair, because they believe in nature and it is the nature of hair to grow, so they let it grow. Thick dreadlocks have to be taken care of very carefully. They are washed with black soil. They are dried in sunlight. Nagas also decorate their dreadlocks. Some decorate them with flowers, some with Rudraksha and some with pearl garlands and like dreadlocks, beards are also the identity of Naga Sadhus. It also has to be cared like dreadlocks.

"Naga Sadhus have to follow some rules as well. For example, they have to put in absolute faith in the Guru Mantra they receive after their Diksha. All their penance in future is dependent on this guru mantra only. They do not bow down before anybody and they greet others with the mantra - 'Om Namo Narayan.'"

Rumi closed her laptop. Actually, she was quite tired. The incessant thought of Naga Sadhus had started to dominate her day and night, no doubt it raised a curiosity in her mind to know more about them, but on the other hand she was also tense about submitting her research paper on time. She could not delay any further.

"When I met the Naga Sadhus, the first thing I noticed was that some were soft hearted while some were arrogant. The appearance of some Naga Sadhu was so scary that I was afraid to even go near them. I am sorry, I did not say this with the intention of ridiculing them, but for a moment it felt like that. But the mind of these Naga sannyasis is as pure as that of children. I have seen that they are always creating a lot of noise in their arena. Their monastery is always resonating with their antics," said Sridhar.

"Shridhar, when we saw the Naga Sadhus for the first time, we were frightened too. Our meeting happened in that cave where there was hardly any light. So don't feel sorry," Shekhar said, agreeing with him.

Rumi got goosebumps as she remembered that moment. But one should not forget how unbearable, laborious, tough and difficult their journey of life is. In today's time when everyone wants to live a comfortable and luxurious life, it is almost impossible for any worldly person to give up material pleasures and become a Naga Sadhu. The training of Naga Sadhus is inspired by the yogic process, but still it cannot be compared to the unbearable conditions that a Naga Sadhu has to go through.

Seeing her in deep thought, Shekhar put his hand on her shoulder. He can understand that she often goes through dilemmas while writing the topic she has chosen to write about, many questions arise in her mind, which trouble her. But he knew that his research paper will give rise to a new perspective towards Naga Sadhus.

❑

19

The Ultimate Goal - Salvation

"When did you go to the Kumbh Mela?" Rumi asked Shridhar after dinner. It was half past nine. Her mother and father had already gone to sleep. She was very impressed by Shridhar's information. Although he was an engineer he had the views of a scholar.

"I went to Nasik–Trimbakeshwar a long time ago. At that time, I had no intentions to make a documentary film. I was just wandering around but the whole ambience of that place impressed me so much that I decided to make a film. You must be aware that among the Kumbh and Simhastha fairs held in four cities of the country, the Trimbakeshwar - Nashik Kumbh is different, unique and wonderful in many ways. In this the royal bath takes place in two cities. That is, Shaivite sanyasis take a royal bath in Kushavarta Kund, the place where Godavari appears, in the city of Jyotirlinga Trimbakeshwar Shiva, while Vaishnav Vairagi saints take a royal dip in the holy stream of Godavari at Ram Ghat in Nashik, the city of Panchavati, the place of exile of Lord Rama.

"It is recorded in the pages of history that during the rule of Peshwas in the 18th century in Maharashtra the Shaiva sanyasis and Vaishnav Vairagis were involved in a violent conflict with each other on the issue of first royal bath. For decades the Peshwas banned the royal ceremony of Simhast. Then, after an agreement with the saints and sages the Peshwa rulers arranged for the royal bath of Shaivite ascetics in Trimbakeshwar, the city of Shiva, and the royal bath of Vaishnavite ascetics in Panchvati, the place of Lord Rama's exile, and Simhastha began again with its dignity and glory.

"It was there that I got to know that as per the Indian astronomy the Nashik Kumbh is organised when Jupiter (Vrihaspati) and Sun (Surya) are both located in Leo zodiac (Singh rashi) and that is why it is also known as the Simhast Kumbh. The radiance and the atmosphere felt like an uncanny music. For a moment I felt as if I was in a city of hippies. I met Mohan Baba. I saw him applying ash. He told me 'I have been in devotion of Bholenath for five years only. I never had an aim to become a sadhu or a Naga Sadhu. My only aim was to meet Bhole Baba. I started engrossing in devotion and japa. I penanced at different places and immersed myself completely in Bhagwan Bholenath. I took a vow to remain silent and not to speak for 12 years. That was my period of Sadhana. My goal was to not speak good or evil to anybody. I just wanted to pray. In this Kalyuga, it is the silence which has the power to speak about everything. Maunam Sarvartha Sadhanam. Just understand your spirituality, serve your parents and live your life for the welfare of people.'

"When I asked him why do you penance so hard? What is the point in inflicting so much pain on yourself, to which he replied 'the only reason behind this is to attain Moksha. Attachment is what makes us unhappy and do not allow to choose the path of Moksha. We need to practice detachment. Whatever makes your body happy, give it up. Do not do any such thing that seeds any attachment for the body or anything.'

"To be honest, even after reaching Simhastha Kumbh Mela and getting the idea of making a film, I did not know what I would make the film about. During that time, I got to witness unique qualities and characteristics of different types of Naga Sadhus. Some had long hair while other had long nails. I saw that they were performing different stunts. They do this before going for the royal bath. Some were performing death defying acts and stunts. Naga Sadhus believe that such stunts will prove that they have surrendered before Shiva. They believe that these acts will strengthen their soul and heart. Some of the activities included inserting sharp objects in their sensitive parts and standing straight for hours. Some Sadhus buried themselves under the ground for several days. Their world is very strange. They astonished the worldly people by showing their stunts."

Rumi and Shekhar were listening to Shridhar very attentively. It was as if they had transcended into a different world.

Shekhar said, "It is impossible to imagine Kumbha until you witness it with your own eyes."

"You are absolutely right Shekhar," Shridhar said, "I had witnessed scenes which I had never seen before, I had the opportunity to meet such divine souls whom I had never even thought about. It felt like I had witnessed the ocean of emotions. It is the biggest celebration that is organised on the earth. It is a window to peep into the heart of India. Kumbha Mela is a celebration of joy. It is a search for a fundamental truth even amidst the costumes, language, culture and innumerable differences of different sects. I felt as if I have transcended into a spiritual world. I felt moments that I had never felt before. It is very difficult to explain those experience, but may be through my film you guys would be able to live it too."

"We too should go to the Kumbha Mela Shekhar," Rumi said all of a sudden, "Everybody knows that more than five crore people from all corners of India visit there. All differences are erased once you reach there. Kumbha is an opportunity to free yourself from all the worries and enjoy the suavity of life. This celebration which gives you an experience of grandeur is a bunch of festivities for the human life. Isn't it interesting that the group of sages, Sanyasis and Sadhus arrive here and set up their camps under the banners of their sects."

Hearing this Shridhar said, "I have tried to show something similar in my film. All kinds of sadhus and saints who live in forests, caves, caverns and mountains or who run ashrams and akharas and who travel with the resolve of 'Charaiveti-Charaiveti' gather to celebrate the Kumbh festival without any invitation. They gather and set up camps among men with families. I have experienced nectar pouring in the Sadhana, discussion of knowledge and satsang of these saints and mahatmas. If you look at it traditionally, this organization of sadhus is the objective of this mela. During the times when there were no cell phones then they could not contact each other and used to meet in the mela.

"The Kumbha amazes you with its diversity as well. From north to east and west to south, from Ganga to Kaveri, From Himalayas to Sahyadri, streams of knowledge and consciousness converge in the Kumbh. This Amrit Mahakumbh is the soul of Sanatan tradition. Kumbh is a national sentiment. I often say that those who want to know India, can understand it through Kumbh. To understand India, it is necessary to understand Sanatan Dharma and there is no better opportunity than Kumbh Mela to understand Sanatan Dharma.

"It is common belief that Kumbh means only to take a dip in the river but that is not correct. I got to see a lively atmosphere, there was a bustle all around me. One can witness many activities throughout the day. In one pandal thousands were being fed while on another pandal two thousand would be preparing food. The pandals were also very grand. Some pandals were very simple. I think such diversity and inclusion of intense energy cannot be seen anywhere else. In my view, Kumbh Mela is the most deeply touching experience on earth. It creates a spiritual atmosphere, which is constantly being purified by the holy vibrations of countless saints. Kumbh is a symbol of awakening of collective consciousness. Kumbh is a great sacrifice for the welfare of the living beings and the world." While saying this, Shridhar became emotional.

Rumi and Shekhar felt as if they were entering into a spiritual world while listening.

"Shridhar, if you are getting late then you can go," Shekhar said.

"I will sit for a while." At dinner Rumi said, " I have included a chapter on Khumbh Mela in my research paper. Although I have collected a lot of information, but Shridhar can I add what all you had mentioned?"

"Absolutely," Shridhar said excited.

Rumi opened her laptop and started reading the chapter on Kumbh Mela, which she had written. "Kumbh Mela is held on the banks of four holy rivers. In the east it is held in Prayag on the banks of the Ganga River. In the west it is held in Ujjain on the banks of the Shipra River. In the north it is held in Haridwar on the banks of the Ganga River and in the south it is held in Nashik on the banks of the Godavari River. It takes place once in three years and since it is being held at four different places it is held at one place once in twelve years. Every three years a temporary city is established with full grandeur and after a month it sets out on a journey to the next place. After travelling for twelve years this temporary city comes and settles at the same place. That is why Kumbh Mela can also be called a nomadic tourist city. Traditionally this Kumbh has been organised by the Akharas.

"Kumbh Mela is timeless. There is no incident which marks the beginning of Kumbh Mela. Although the oldest mention about Kumbh Mela in history is found during the reign of Emperor Harshvardhan (612 - 647 AD), which is recorded by famous Chinese traveller Huen Tsang in his travelogue in the seventh century - 'Emperor Harshvardhan, like his predecessors, used to first dedicate all his wealth collected for five years in front of the statue of Lord Buddha in the holy land of Prayag. Then he used to distribute that wealth to the local priests, then to the priests from outside, then to the prominent scholars, then to the heretics and finally to the widows, the helpless, the beggars, the handicapped, the poor and the Sadhus. In this way, after distributing all his wealth and food-stock, the emperor used to donate his precious royal crown, jewelled necklace and even the clothes he was wearing. In the end, after giving away everything, the king would happily say, 'I have given away everything I have to a treasury that will never become empty.'

"This description shows that Emperor Harshvardhan, like his predecessors, used to organize this Mahadaan Mahotsav in Prayag on the banks of Triveni (Prayag) in the sixth year. But nowhere has it been proved that this event was called Kumbh or it was started by Harshvardhan. Because in this description, Harshvardhan has been described as the imitator of his predecessors. All these facts show that in the Buddhist period, the prevalent form of Kumbh must have changed and come in the form of Mahadaan festival, which later the Acharyas of Vedic Sanatan Dharma must have given a reorganized form and declared Kumbh festival.

"It is said that on the occasion of Kumbh mela in year 1621 there was a violent conflict between the Udasin and Vairagi Sadhus over the issue of taking the first bath. At that time the then Mughal emperor Jahangir had visited the site himself. But, in his desire to see the fight between the Sadhus, he forbade the royal soldiers from interfering in the fight. On the occasion of the Haridwar Kumbh Mela in 1666, the emperor and Aurangzeb's soldiers attacked, which were countered by the sadhus and saints along with the Naga sanyasis. Witnessing the religious banner of the sages, the Marthas in the Mughal sena switched sides and joined the group of saints. Aurangzeb had to face humiliating defeat. There are evidences of conflict between Sanyasis and Vairagis during the Kumbh mela in 1690 AD. Referring to the Haridwar Kumbh Mela in 1760, the English author Wilson has written in his memoirs, 'There was a fierce fight between the sanyasis and the vairagis. From this Kumbh Mela, the Vaishnav Mahatmas stopped going to Kumbh. These people started celebrating their Kumbh festival in Vrindavan. Later, when the British took control of Haridwar, the vairagis again started coming to Haridwar Kumbh, but even today, according to that tradition, Vaishnavi Akharas take their first bath in Vrindavan and not in Haridwar Kumbh. During the second and third baths, people of Ani Akharas take a royal bath along with other Akharas. Vaishnav saints take the third bath alone instead of taking a bath on Shivratri. On the occasion of Haridwar Kumbh in 1796, the main reason for the fight between Vaishnavs and Sikh saints was that the saints of Nirmal sect, under the protection of the King of Patiala, also wanted to take a royal bath in Kumbh. But other sects did not allow them to take a royal bath with the

Akhara. As a result, the agitated saints of Nirmal sect established Nirmal Akhara under agreements with other saints, and gave it recognition and allowed it to participate in the royal bath with them.

"Historian Jadu Nath Sarkar believes the time around 13th century to be the beginning of Kumbh mela. He has talked about Kumbh while referring to the incident of Naga ascetics winning over Vaishnavs and Vairagis in 1253. Historians have also mentioned the presence of Chaitanya Mahaprabhu in the Kumbh of Prayag in 1514 AD.

"Kumbh festival has been celebrated for centuries in four cities of India, which are situated on the banks of different rivers in four directions. But there are no historical and authentic documents available in written form except religious texts like Vedas, Puranas etc. Mahant Lalpuriji has written in his book 'Dashnam Naga Sanyaasi and Shri Panchayat Akhara Mahanirvani' in the chapter titled 'Vikas of Kumbh festival' that, 'There is also a view regarding the development of Kumbh mela in its current form that during the golden age of Indian history, the Gupta Empire (320 - 600 AD), just as the Puranic literature came in its re-edited form, similarly, on the basis of Puranic and astrological literature, the place and time of Kumbh festivals were permanently determined and developed in its current form.' But this will be considered only as an opinion. It is not a factual or authentic historical statement. Because the decision of place and time has been going on in this form since much before the Gupta Empire, so it is useless to say anything in this regard. Rather, there is a need for deep historical research in this subject. But it is very ironical that historians have ignored it by considering it merely a fair or festival of saints and sages."

"How is it decided when and where the Kumbh Mela will be held?" Shekhar asked.

"It is decided on the basis of astronomical events. During these periods, the energy is concentrated in spiritual form, so this event is also called a divine event. The place and date of the Kumbh Mela are decided with the help of the position of the Sun, Moon and Jupiter in different zodiac signs. These astronomical events also have symbolic meanings here. In Sanatan Dharma, the Sun is considered the soul, the Moon is considered the mind and Jupiter is considered the god of religion. When religion is followed, the mind gets purified and the purification of the mind opens the door to self-realization. That is why Kumbh Mela holds a special significance for seekers," Rumi said.

After dropping Shridhar outside, Rumi said, "Shekhar, why do you ruin your sleep because of me. You should also go."

"Anything for you," Shekhar smiled and kissed Rumi's cheeks. She blushed.

"I actually want to hear the story of Samudra Manthan. I will leave after listening to that," Shekhar said while lying down on the sofa. Rumi kept a plate of dry fruits in front of him and said, "Eat these. You will get some energy."

"My energy level increases just by looking at you."

"It will be better to tell you a story before you start getting romantic," Rumi said while caressing his hair.

"The gods and demons decided to churn the ocean and share all the gems that came out of it. The most valuable gem that came out of the churning of the ocean was Amrit (nectar). There was a fight between the gods and demons to get it, so to save Amrit from the demons, Lord Vishnu gave that vessel or pot to his vehicle Garuda. When the demons tried to snatch that vessel from Garuda, a few drops of Amrit spilled from that vessel and fell in Allahabad, Nashik, Haridwar and Ujjain. Since then, Kumbh Mela is organized at these places every 12 years. The Kumbh Mahaparva bath takes place in the four holy places mentioned above when the Sun, Moon and Jupiter are in the same zodiac signs in which they were located at the time of protecting the Amrit Ghat. Guru Brihaspati protected the Amrit Kumbh from the demons, the Sun saved the pitcher from breaking and the Moon saved the Amrit from the pot from falling, that is why these three have a deep connection with the Kumbh Mela."

Shekhar probably dozed off while listening. Should I wake him up or let him sleep... Rumi was thinking when her mother came. She had probably got up to go to the washroom. She said softly, "Let him sleep. Get a blanket for him."

Rumi looked at the sleeping Shekhar and went to her room.

❑

20
The Glory of Kumbh

Even though the tradition of Kumbh Mela is becoming limited to symbolism today, but definitely there must have been a time when the coming together of sadhus and sages in such a manner, sitting together with families from near and far, reviewing various subjects related to religious scriptures and discussing philosophical questions and generously donating food and clothes, as well as performing rituals like Yagya, was not only very effective but also beneficial for the entire society.

It is written in 'Jhansi Gazetteer' that in year 1751 Ahmad Khan Bangas defeated the Wazir of Delhi and Nawab of Awadh, Safdarjung and surrounded the fort of Allahabad. He was about to capture the town but the Kumbh of Prayag arrived. A grand congregation of spiritual people from across the country and beyond was held with their participation. A huge group of Naga Sadhus also arrived there in the leadership of Rajendra Giri. According to various accounts the number of these sadhus was in between six thousand and fifty thousand. They first completed their religious rituals performed during the Kumbh festival and then took up weapons. From February to April, they fought with the army of Ahmed Khan Bangas, defeated him and protected the city of Prayag (Allahabad). This narration nowhere proves that Adi Shankaracharya established the present form of Kumbh mela. Moreover, during the period of Adi Shankaracharya, apart from Naga ascetics Shri Sampradaya (Vaishnav) and Udasin sects where in existence as well. Their Acharyas used to come for Kumbh bath with their followers and saints. Therefore, it does not seem to be historical to say that the present form of Kumbh festival was propounded by Adi Shankaracharya. Yes, it is a different matter that the Vedic Sanatan Dharma upliftment work done by Adi Shankaracharya has its own special significance. No Sanatan follower can ignore his work. It is written in the book 'Dabistan' of 1050 AD that 'In 1050 AD, a fierce battle took place between the Vaishnavas and the Sannyasis in the Kumbh Mela of Haridwar in which thousands of Vaishnavas and Sannyasis were killed. The remaining Vaishnavas and Sannyasis gave up Tilak and Tulsi Mala to save their lives and disguised themselves as 'Kanfata Jogis', a sect of sanyasis who get their ears pierced.

It is believed that taking a bath during the Kumbh mela clear all sins and evils and grants salvation. It is also believed that during the period of Kumbh the water in Ganga is filled with positive energy and during the Kumbh the water is filled with positive electromagnetic radiations from the sun, the moon and Jupiter.

Rumi was sitting and writing when Prof Vachaspati entered his study. He took a quick glance at her notes and said, "It is important that in your research paper you mention about the Kumbh Mela in detail because the Akharas and the Naga Sadhus have very close connection with the Kumbh mela."

"Yes Sir."

She began to write, The word Kumbh is derived from Kumbhak which means a vessel filled with the nectar of immortality. This word is related to taking a bath in that holy water hence taking a bath in that period becomes so important. During the Kumbh mela, there are five most important days for bath and three of them fall in the category of royal bath. On the day of royal bath, all the thirteen Akharas take a holy dip following a prescribed order. They hold a procession which is a spectacular sight in itself, as the head of the group of sadhus sits on elephants, horses and chariots which are beautifully decorated. There is a special order of the royal bath of the Akharas in the Kumbh Mela. In the Shahi Snan, Juna, Ahwaan and Ani Akharas take bath first. After that Niranjani and Anand Akhara take a dip of faith in the holy Ganga. After this, the sadhus and saints of Mahanirvani and Atal Akhara take Kumbh bath at the Brahmakund of Har Ki Pauri.'

'The first thing to happen in the Kumbh is the Nagar Pravesh in which the sadhus arrive on elephants, horses, carriages and trolleys etc. In a way it is also a display of power. Afte the Nagar Pravesh, a religious banner is placed. To make the religious flag, the entire wood of a 52-yard tree is brought from the forest. The condition for selecting the tree is that it should not be cut from anywhere and there should not be any nail in it. The flag is brought from the forest and put on it. After this, the religious flag is hoisted with the chanting of mantras.'

'The sadhus can return to their tents only after the completion of this ceremony. The raising of religious flag marks the beginning of Kumbh. Next day the procession takes place. In this procession these people carry their gods, spears and swords. They are led by their chief Mahamandaleshwar and the remining sadhus walk behind him according to the precedence order. In a way this procession is the tradition to display the military power.

'The grandeur of the Naga Sadhus in the Kumbh bath was like that of kings, and because of this it is called the royal bath. When the procession of the Mahanirvani Akhara is taken out, the flag of the Akhara is at the front. Behind it, a group of Naga ascetics move ahead showing their skills. There was a statue of the revered Kapil Muni mounted on the chariot, on which the Mahatma waves a 'Chanvar'. In between, the sadhus and mahatmas riding on the chariot shower flowers by dipping them in water on the devotees standing in the queue for darshan. The Naga Sadhus also display their war skills by stopping at various places with their weapons. On both sides of the road, two Naga saints ride on two horses and play drums. The Sadhus, mahatmas, saints and Nagas walk in between them.

'Every akhara has a fixed and allotted time. This time can vary from thirty minutes to one hour. The time depends upon the size of the respective procession. Even the routes taken for the royal bath are taken care of here. This is done so that the members of the rival Akharas are kept apart from each other, and clashes can be avoided.'

"Sir, please tell something about the relation of zodiac signs with Kumbh as well."

Prof Vachaspati moved his glasses and said "According to the beliefs of Hinduism, Kumbh Mela is organized when Jupiter enters Aquarius and the Sun enters Aries. The Kumbh Mela of Prayag holds the greatest importance among all the fairs. Kumbh means – Kalash or a pot, in astrology, Aquarius is also the symbol. The mythological belief of Kumbh Mela is related to Amrit Manthan, about which you have already written. There is also an astrological explanation of Kumbh Mela, according to which it seems that Kumbh Mela is related to the religious place at the time of Kumbh - Yoga. To determine the exact date and time of Kumbh Yoga, the position and conjunction of planets like Sun, Moon, Jupiter and Saturn is taken into consideration. When Sun and Moon are in Capricorn and Jupiter is in Taurus, then Kumbh is held in Prayag. When Jupiter is in Aquarius and Sun in Aries and Moon in Sagittarius, then Kumbh is organised in Haridwar. When Jupiter is in Leo and Sun and Moon are in Cancer, then Kumbh Mela is organised in Nashik. When Jupiter is in Leo and Sun and Moon are in Aries, then Kumbh is celebrated in Ujjain.

"Kumbh Mela plays a pivotal spiritual role in the country, which has a mesmerizing effect on Indians. The event encompasses the science of astronomy, astrology, spirituality, ritual traditions and social and cultural customs and practices, making it extremely rich in knowledge. Since it is held in four different cities of India, it involves various social and cultural activities, making it a culturally diverse festival. The knowledge and skills related to the tradition are transmitted through ancient religious manuscripts, oral traditions, historical travelogues and texts produced by eminent historians. However, the teacher-student relationship of sadhus in ashrams and akharas is the most important way of imparting and preserving the knowledge and skills related to the Kumbh Mela."

Rumi continued recording everything. She sensed Prof Vachaspati's busy schedule and left for home. She also had to read Kirat's diary whose many pages are still unread. She started searching for what was written about Kumbh mela. It was not much but only a few pages mentioned them. Rumi began reading them. 'It seems that the Kumbh Mela must have started first in Haridwar, when after twelve years Jupiter is positioned in

Aquarius and the Sun is positioned in Aries. Such an astronomical coincidence has been mentioned in the Naradiya Purana, according to which this is a holy time for bathing in the Ganga. Later, this festival started being celebrated in Prayag, Ujjain and Nashik as well. The tradition of bathing at the confluence of Ganga, Yamuna and Saraswati in the month of Magh in Prayag is very old. On the occasion of Kumbh Melas, the most intimate level of social-religious interaction takes place between sadhus and householders. As a collective ritual, Kumbh Mela is a symbolic expression of the fundamental contract between caste-based society and religious institutions in Indian culture. The colourful procession of the Akhara and the tradition of royal bath act as a powerful catalyst to generate social consciousness among the common people and thus boost the morale of the society.

'The unbroken tradition of Maha Kumbh festival, which has been going on for centuries, has been a symbol of the immense feeling of unity inherent in Indian culture. Where saints, sages and monks of all religions, great scholars of philosophy, Mahants and Peethadheeshwars of big monasteries gather, the rich and poor, small and big, kings and paupers of all sections of the people gather with great enthusiasm from north-south and east-west. Kumbh festival becomes such a huge festival in which linguistic differences and regional religious or sectarian narrowness automatically disappear.

'As far as the akharas are concerned, Kumbh mela provides them with a platform to propagate their religion and philosophy as well as to display their grandeur. The people who have gathered from every corner of the country benefit from the knowledge and wisdom of the learned saints and Mahamandaleshwars of the Akhara through their discourses. There is no doubt that the Ashrams, Mathas and Akharas are important parts of the mechanism of propagating religious faith in India on the occasion of Kumbh Melas.

'The Kumbh Mela is important for the akharas not only from a spiritual point of view but a political one as well. Akharas are the panchayati organisation and they believe in a democratic system. Many officials are appointed for the smooth functioning and management of these huge organisations. These officials are elected unanimously only on the occasion of Kumbh Melas and Ardh Kumbh Melas.

'I was surprised to see that the bhandaras given by various akharas on the occasion of Kumbh Mela are also unique. They too have a significance. I understood that these bhandaras are a symbol of love and brotherhood which are organised by the akhadas either alone or together. These bhandaras are of two types. The first type of bhandara is called Vyashti bhandara, in which a few people are invited. The second type of bhandara is called Samashti bhandara, in which a large number of people are invited. At some places, several thousand sadhus are invited. The time of the bhandara is fixed and the holy food is ready before that. All the Mahamandaleshwars arrive with their assistants and sit at the designated place and some of them also give discourses, which other sadhus listen to attentively. After the discourses are over, the Mahamandaleshwars are worshipped with camphor and garlands. The bugle is blown and the sadhus and saints chant 'Om Namah Parvati Pataye, Har Har Mahadev'. At this time, the 15th chapter of the Gita is also read. After this, Prasad is distributed, which is usually made of various types of wheat sweets, curd, rabri and vegetables.

'I came to know one more thing that in Kumbh, every sadhu has to give dakshina according to his capacity. It is called 'pukar'. The bigger the Sadhu, the bigger the Pukar. Not only this, I saw that the youth have a lot of expectations from Naga Sadhus. Some discuss with them to get rid of unemployment, while some ask for solutions to worldly problems. I also saw parents asking questions that their child is not interested in studies. And this was a very surprising thing for me. Even though Naga Sadhus follow the path of renunciation, but most of their devotees are worldly. At that time, I did not know that I too would someday become their devotee and follow their path.'

Rumi closed her diary. Kirat's face flashed before her eyes. He had gone to learn about Naga Sadhus and was inspired by their lives and became a Naga Sadhu himself. Even after knowing how difficult it is to become a Naga Sadhu. Truly, a person's will can empower him to achieve so much!

❑

21
The Sadhus Deserve Respect

"Rumi, if you want, you can end your research paper with the mention of Ram temple in Ayodhya. Naga Sadhus have played an important role in the struggle for construction of this temple. This case was fought by a Naga Sadhu," Prof Vachaspati said on the phone.

"But sir, will it be correct to mention this? Won't anybody raise any objections?" Rumi was confused.

"What is there to object now? The temple of Shree Ram is now built and Ram Lalla has been placed there. Naga Sadhus have sacrificed a lot to save Ayodhya."

"Of course."

Rumi kept thinking about it for quite some time. Then she had to take the help of internet. She was amazed to see how the Naga Sadhus had placed their life on the line to protect the Ram Janmabhoomi from foreign invaders. Many Naga soldiers like Devideen Pandey and Swami Maheshanand and Naga Sadhu leaders like Sant Balaramacharya and Baba Vaishnav Das fought in 76 clashes and gave their life to protect the Ram temple. Sant Balanand and Mandas fought the Mughal, Turk and Afghan armies for decades to save Ayodhya. After that, a legal battle for Lord Ram's temple continued for decades. The case went on from civil court to High Court and Supreme Court. Hundreds of witnesses appeared in the Supreme Court, many documents were kept as evidence and finally the decision came in favour of the Hindu.

She searched again to know more about that lawyer who fought this case. She came to know that 'The famous lawyer Karunesh Shukla, who is a Naga Sadhu, who fought the case of Shri Ram Janmabhoomi on behalf of the Hindu side, has formally studied law. Then he fought the case for Ram Lalla. Now he is the main petitioner in the Shri Krishna Janmabhoomi dispute of Mathura. Karunesh Shukla, originally from Basti in Uttar Pradesh, received his early education in Saraswati Shishu Mandir. He says that 'there was a very religious - spiritual atmosphere in my family from the very beginning. When my grandmother used to go for Kalpavas, I would definitely go with her. Grandmother often used to go to Ayodhya and Banaras too. When she returned from Ayodhya, she would always say sadly that it hurts a lot to see God in a tent. There is not even a temple for him. In the 1990s, when the Ram Janmabhoomi movement was moving towards a decisive battle, my grandmother and mother sent me to Hanumangarhi for Ram's work. They wanted me to stay in Ayodhya and serve God.

'After completing my eighth standard I came to Hanumangarhi on the orders of my family. Here I learned wrestling and took initiation by staying at Mahant Harihar Das Pehlwan's ashram. Here I studied Ramcharitmanas and all the Vedas and Puranas and then became a Naga Sadhu. However, my studies continued even after becoming a Sadhu.'

'After coming to Hanumangarhi, I understood the essence of Shri Ram Janmabhoomi and this fight more deeply. My guru and family members wanted someone to fight Ram Lalla's case and plead in the court. For this, they chose me.

'I studied law from Kanpur in the year 2011. After this, I appeared in the court as Respondent No. 14 on behalf of Shri Mahant Dharmdas Nirvani Akhara in the Shri Ram Janmabhoomi dispute. I used to cry whenever I saw Lord Ram in tent. Now after a struggle of centuries when the God is coming to his temple. It seems me that studying law has borne its fruit. I might appear wearing a black coat but I too am a Naga Sadhu and follow all the rules and rituals.

Rumi was astonished to read this.

"A Naga Sadhu fought the case for Ram Janmabhoomi!" She said while have tea in the evening with her parents.

They too were amazed to hear this.

"You can call him. You will get more information about him," his father gave the idea.

"Good idea papa! I can get the number from the internet." Rumi went to her room.

She found the number but it took her some time to connect with Karunesh Shukla. Initially it was Rumi who had to answer a lot of questions and finally after he was satisfied, Karunesh Shukla came to the phone.

"Sorry, you had to answer to a lot of people. We Naga Sadhus have to follow so many rules. Tell me, what do you want to know?" Karunesh Shukla said politiely?"

"A Naga Sadhu in a black coat? Did nobody say anything to you?"

"It is God's grace. Many people ask me how did you become a lawyer being a Naga Sadhu? My answer is always that I am what God wants me to be."

"Why did you become a Naga Sadhu?"

"My whole family comes from Basti (Uttar Pradesh). Being from a Brahmin family, there used to be a lot of devotion in my home. I too used to participate in worships and prayers in my home. My mother wanted that a member of our household should go to Ayodhya and serve Lord Ram. I followed my mother's wish and went to Ayodhya. There I lived in Hanumangarhi, did worship and then took initiation. Stayed in Mahant Harishankar Das Pehlwan's ashram and studied wrestling, Ramcharitmanas and Vedanta in depth. Along with this, I became a Naga Sadhu."

"You study law even after you became a Naga Sadhu? Why? Did no one stop you?"

"My family wanted me to serve Ram. So I got a way to serve him this way. No one stopped me because I was on the way to protect the Dharma and it is the duty of a Naga Sadhu to protect the Dharma."

Rumi hung up the phone as Karunesh Shukla said that now it is his meditation time.

In conclusion Rumi wrote, 'Only a few lucky people can become Naga Sadhus. The strongest commitment makes a Naga. The process of achieving Naga status is very difficult and the practice is so tough that it cannot be compared to the toughest preparations of any army around the world. The training of the army around the world is inspired by the training and yoga process of Naga Sadhus, but still it cannot be compared to the unbearable painful conditions that a Naga Sadhu has to go through.

'Naga Sadhus go through a painful and tiring process to test their self - control. They increase their penance by testing their limits to the extreme. Naga Sadhus are the living great men of the world. The Hindus of India are very grateful to the ancient Naga Sadhus and Sri Adi Shankaracharya. We should respect Naga Sadhus.'

"I have to return Kirat's diary to Mahamandleshwar Girinathji in Ujjain," Rumi said to Shekhar after submitting her research paper to Prof. Vachaspati.

"Tell me, when do we have to go to Ujjain?" Shekhar asked."

"As soon as I get the ticket."

Both of them had returned after returning Kirat's precious possession. They had not only learnt a lot about Naga Sadhus, but had also understood life in a better way. It is not easy to remove the notions that our society forms about anyone without thinking.

But Rumi was confident that her paper would surely change the perception about Naga Sadhus and society would understand their long standing commitment and value in the society.